AFRICAN VISAS

AFRICAN VISAS

A Novella and Stories

MARIA THOMAS

SOHO

The following stories have been previously published: "Back Bay to the Bundu" in The New Yorker *and "Makonde Carvers" in* Story *magazine.*

Published by
Soho Press, Inc.
853 Broadway
New York, NY 10003

Library of Congress Cataloging-in-Publication Data
Thomas, Maria, 1941–1989
African visas : a novella and stories / Maria Thomas.
p. cm.
ISBN 0–939149–76–1
1. Americans—Africa—Fiction. 2. Africa—Fiction. I. Title.
PS3570.H5735A37 1991
813'.54—dc20 91–3829
CIP

Manufactured in the United States
10 9 8 7 6 5 4 3 2 1

Book design and composition by
The Sarabande Press

PUBLISHER'S NOTE

In deference to the author's preference, the capital of Ethiopia is spelled throughout this text as *Addis Abeba* which most closely approximates its pronunciation in Amharic.

[exit fool]

Poor naked wretches, wheresoe'er you are,
That bide the pelting of this pitiless storm,
How shall your houseless heads and unfed sides,
Your loop'd and window'd raggedness, defend you
From seasons such as these? O, I have ta'en
Too little care of this! Take physic pomp;
Expose thyself to feel what wretches feel,
That thou mayst shake the superflux to them,
And show the heavens more just.

KING LEAR, ACT III, SCENE 4

THE JIRU ROAD 1

BACK BAY TO THE BUNDU 127

THE BLOND MASAI 147

THE VISIT 165

MAKONDE CARVERS 187

MY MERMAID 203

ETHIOPIA 221

THE JIRU ROAD

I had been earmarked as scholar bait and spinster material as far back as the second grade. It was not only a matter of the brains I had but of the looks I didn't have. During those early years of bedtime stories, I remember my mother featured the one about the ugly duckling that grew up to be a beautiful swan. I grew, oh my yes, I grew and didn't stop until I was six-foot-two. But none of it, as far as I could tell, was beautiful.

I reckon I joined the Peace Corps because I was trying to avoid conscription. Not into the army, like my draft dodging male counterparts, and not into marriage, like my reluctant female counterparts. It was conscription into American life. I was just a kid trying to sneak out of the twentieth century. Little things informed against me. Whenever I saw a tag ordering me to dry clean something, I washed it for spite. I resented my bandaged thumbs, victims of pop-top cans. I hated finding cheap towels in my box of Tide. So I left. I went away to where I thought the big battles would be with the elements, where no energy had to be wasted peeling the stuck plastic off individually wrapped pieces of cheese.

After college I filled up on Peace Corps literature and sent an application to their offices in Washington, D.C. I wrote that I would only go to Bengal. I related in my essay that I had a special interest in floods because I was a flood survivor myself, had lived through the devastation of a Kansas deluge as a child. But (like the Spanish speaking applicants from the Southwest who'd pleaded for Latin America) I got sent to Africa.

In the offices of the Peace Corps in Washington, application forms toss around like so many messages sealed in bottles and sent out to sea. After months of rising and falling with the tides and drifting in and out on currents, my bottle washed up on the desk of one Yvonne Lumpkins, who placed an urgent person-to-person, long distance phone call to me. A person of my skills, she said, (I had been an art major), was needed right away in a place called Jiru. In the Horn of Africa.

"I want to go to Bengal," I told her.

"Everyone wants to go there," she muttered. "Well, we've stopped our programs in Bengal."

"Well, then India as a last resort."

"If it's one or the other I can't help you. This is the Africa desk."

She sounded angry, as though I had said something offensive.

"You think Peace Corps is a little free travel arrangement, is that it? You want to find your way to some ashram? Smoke a little dope? Find a guru? Study Buddhism on the government, is that it? I'm getting sick of you kids."

I stammered something apologetic.

"Well, get your old man to buy you a ticket to India." She hung up.

I suspect she tossed my application back into the paper sea, where it fell into a whirlpool, reached bottom somewhere, and was spit up again right back on her desk. She didn't recognize it the second time around and called again, once again urgently. Again this place called Jiru. This time I said I would go. By now I was living at home and I was desperate. As I hung up that phone I had a niggling premonition that my adulthood would follow this pattern, a series of last resorts and desperate alternatives. I didn't know that I was going to love it in Jiru.

1. I started on my way alone

The first time I went to Jiru, a bus trip of two days and then half a day's walk from the capital, I started on my way alone. At that time the Peace Corps believed in immersion, in going native from the start. In three months of training I had come a long way: had embraced a new landscape, lacy with tall eucalyptus, glowing with strange flowers; had learned a new language that popped with explosive letters; had survived a bout of dysentery which landed me in a hospital; had learned to drink honey beer and tell time by counting the hours from sun up (instead of from noon); had learned how to dance the *iskistis* which features a rhythmic pumping of the shoulders, and an accordion movement with the knees, accompanied by a hissing zuck-zuck sound made through the teeth. I was a natural when it came to the *iskistis* and quickly acquired a taste for honey beer. But as I climbed on that bus to Jiru, I didn't have so much as an inkling about where I was going or what I faced. It was as unclear as my naked vision, a blur of naiveté and expectation. I had cause to distrust my feelings. Disappointment, I had learned, often followed expectation, and surprise was only premonition, good or bad. You waited and hoped for the best. I was hoping for the best in Jiru.

I had not been introduced to the network of other volunteers already serving in-country. My own group, all trained and ready like Christian soldiers, had gone marching as to war in separate directions. We were expected to get along on our own. But there was another white face on that bus to Jiru and I went right for it.

It was Wally Martin's. He had very red, very long, very curly hair and he wore a bright green John Deere cap with a button collection on the visor.

"Mind if I have a look at your lenses?" he asked. "Man, you got *some* lenses."

I had heard of boob men and leg men. I had never heard of lens men.

I handed him my glasses. The world blurred. Except for the smell of people who loved to burn incense (even on buses) and who spent most of their time sitting around cook fires made with eucalyptus bark (slightly camphoric), and except for the sound of chickens that were scratching and clucking under the seats of the bus, I would never have known where I was. I could feel my eyes sink in their sockets. Wally Martin appeared doubled, a red fuzz, the John Deere cap like a leaf falling across the autumn of my failing vision.

"They can do wonders with glass," he said. "Through lenses we can see other worlds: small ones, big ones." He returned my sight. "Are you the new vol in Jiru?"

"Yes, my names's Sarah Easterday. People call me Shoulders." I did a bit of the *iskistis,* zuck-zuck.

"I'm Wally Martin," he said. "We're neighbors." Whining nasal music blasted from a nearly ruined cassette player in the front of the bus, so loud that we were prevented from any real conversation. The few words of that song that I could understand told the old story: some unfaithful woman was on the loose in town. Her forlorn lover was calling her his lost orange. To avoid headache, I went to sleep. Wally Martin claimed that I slept through three cases of motion sickness, a divorce, an attempted suicide and two pickpockets caught red-handed in the seat behind us.

We stopped for the night in a town called Makele. We had the choice of sleeping on the bus, in the field next to it, or in one of the rooms built behind the coffeehouses and restaurants clustered near the bus stop.

Wally Martin led the way past pink and fluorescent interiors, and the open doors from which poured the smell of dark coffee and that same pop lament—the weepy boyfriend crying over his lost orange like a pathetic fruit seller—toward three flashing blue lights at the end of a narrow street that marked the entrance to the John F. Kennedy Coffee House and Bar.

Before we ever saw the American advisors, we saw their car, a white Chevy wagon with an American flag and a decal of clasped hands on the driver's door, announcing they had come in friendship and cooperation. On this particular occasion they had come in drunken abandon. They were thumping the table and teasing the girls, one on every knee.

"What's that TAWL DRINK A WATER you got, Wally boy? Ain't you drinkin' HARD stuff tonight?" Before I knew it this loud voiced man had produced a hand for Wally to shake, while the other was reaching up and clamping my shoulder with vigor. "Wha, you must be a new member of the Peace Corpse!" he hooted. "Well, let's us have a welcomin' drink to that. Drinks all around! We have a new Piece in the Corps. Right, Wally ol' boy."

I stared down at the top of this man's head. A bald spot gleamed under wisps of fine yellow hair.

Wally made introductions. The man was Jack Archibald, and "I reckon they call you Sally," he said. His boozy breath formed a cloud under my chin and then came at me from all directions. He pressed me to sit down on the nearest chair while, still standing, he leaned in for a close look. He was wearing glasses at least as thick as mine, and our rims knocked in greeting. The lens over his right eye was blackened so he pulled back, head cocked to one side to give his left eye reign.

"They call me Shoulders," I said.

"Well I'll be damned to hell!" he roared. Drinks were coming around, big, brown bottles of beer. "Grab your beer Shoulders ol' girl and come join us." He rolled away, as fat as he was tall, tipping to the left as he went.

His friend Jack Proctor had a distinguished southwestern air. On his pressed shirt, a bolo tie was secured by a large hunk of marbled turquoise set in heavy silver. When he leaned back to greet us, his big silver belt buckle knocked against the table, and as he shook hands his Zuñi watchband shimmered with turquoise and red coral inlay. A whore, who was bouncing absently on his knee, pulled a pearl gray Stetson from under the table and put it on. He removed it with gentlemanly grace. He wore a patch over his left eye.

"You know who we are?" Jack Archibald bellowed. "Wha, we're a couple a ONE-EYED JACKS!!!!!" The one-eyed jacks crumpled laughing. Wally cracked and chucked and I giggled. "Jest a couple a ol' one-eyed Jacks!"

Archibald by now was out of control, had locked Wally in a full nelson while tears flowed under his glasses. Demure whores, who waited on chairs around the bar, tittered and tweedled. Proctor was having trouble keeping his girl from spilling to the floor.

"You git that, honey?" Archibald asked the girl on Proctor's lap. "Naw, she'll never git it."

From under the table he pulled a gallon of Johnny Walker and slugged some down. Then he whimpered like a kid whose punishment was over, whose crying was done. He wiped his tear stained cheeks, heaved a few last chuckles and sat down, pulling Wally with him. When he recaptured his breath he said, "Now then, tell us about life in the PISS CORE!"

The one-eyed Jacks hoo-haaed and roared, slapping the table with their fists and knocking it with their knees.

"Weeel," Wally drawled, reaching under the table where the Johnny Walker had gone again, "We don't get good booze out where we live."

Archibald hoisted the bottle and shouted, "Drinks all around!!! Drinks on me!!! Bartender!"

Africa seemed to dissolve around him, ceasing to exist. He was making it something else. "To-night," he said, "one-eyed jacks are WILD!" One hand crashed to the table and the other, on pure instinct, reached around behind him to a waiting girl. He pulled her to his lap. "This here is my gal," he said. "Ain't ya honey?"

She nodded.

He patted her gently and kissed her cheek. "You know, no matter how many times I come round here, I can never remember this lil gal's name. What's yer name, honey?"

She whispered something in his ear.

His face screwed up in mock intensity. He whispered, "Same ol'??? What's that you say?" Then his roar, "SAME OL' SNATCH!!!"

The two wild jacks exploded.

More drinks came around. Archibald tossed Scotch into our beer. "Boilermakers," he explained. "I oney sit down with serious drinkers."

Proctor was telling me he was an engineer. He and a crew of ten, fifteen men had built roads all over hell, in Korea, Nam, Malaysia, Indonesia (rubber roads, he said). "Now I'm building a famine road for these people," he said. "Whenever there's a famine, we'll use the road to bring relief in to the people far away from the mainstream." He lit a cigar. He looked like a salesman.

"Sure as shit," Jack Archibald butted in. "Just as sure as shit."

Now, talking to me about a famine relief road was like talking to another famous Kansan about a yellow brick one. I could see it glowing across the desert with caravans of sparkling trucks full of food. I was awestruck—the result of two or three boilermakers—convinced I had found the Wizard of Oz.

"Up 'til now it was them Eye-ties who built all the roads," Archibald was saying. "Say, you ever hear the one about the Eye-ties who stole a garbage truck and went to Florida?"

"Yeh, they thought it was a camper," Wally Martin said.

Archibald whooped and hollered as if he hadn't known the punch line to his own joke. Tears streamed anew from behind his glasses. Then he put on a pout.

"Terrible thing, ain't it?" he sighed. "There jest ain't no luv left in this world. Spics, Eye-ties, niggers. Course, we're all the same underneath. Wha, you won't hear this ol' one-eyed jack say anything bad about another man. No siree. You believe me don't you?"

He landed his lopsided gaze on me.

"Now me, I'm part red Indian. And where I come from, there ain't no Indians but some wild-ass nigger's been in the woodpile. That's how come I say we're all the same underneath. Even Eye-ties. They ain't nothing but niggers turned inside out!"

He howled and belched. Turned to the girl on his knee and asked, "Same ol' snatch? That really your name?" His nose was going from red to purple. Two red patches flamed on his cheeks.

Wally fell asleep, slumped over the table with his chin in his John Deere cap; Proctor, loosening the whores that were clinging to him, strode away to sleep alone after all.

"Sure as shit." Jack Archibald was poking up out of his own snooze and looking at me with one glazed eye.

"Say." He sat bolt upright, "You remind me of my wife. That's what it is. My wife's a tawl drink a water jest like you."

He removed his glasses and rubbed at his tired eyes. One was glass, a poor replica, but it watered and teared as though it were real.

"Yessiree!" He pounded the table and slurped down some more Johnny Walker.

"A TAWL drink a water. Oney," he took my hand in his with a gesture that felt something like regret. "Oney she's—weeeeel, I don't mean to offend now, beauty's oney skin deep like they say." His hand began to feel like melting butter. "Oney she's BUILT! Like a brick shithouse, I'll tell ya! Wha, in those days, I could rest my chin riiiii. . . ." He aimed a finger from his free hand about where I might have had a cleavage if I had had a cleavage, but we were both wobbling so much that by the time he made his move, "riiiiight here!", his finger landed on my liver.

He sank then. "Oh how I luvved that gal, in those days." He sucked at the air. "I really luvved her then. I loved her more than anything. Yes I did." He folded like an origami to the table.

Then he righted himself, looked confused as though he had

spoken in a foreign language and had been misunderstood. "I still luv her now," he said. "Yes I do. But I REALLY luvved her then!" He tried to put his arm around me, but he had no strength. His neck was having trouble supporting his head.

People were starting to sweep up the bar and Wally, coming to, had started talking to the bartender about a place where we could crash. We found our way down a back hallway that had been swabbed so many times with gasoline to keep the bugs down, it smelled like the inside of a Molotov cocktail. The room had the same ambiance. There was no light except when the hall door was opened. We located some beds in it, and fumbled our way to them.

I began to wish I had eaten something. The boilermakers and the bottle of Coke I had taken to try and sober up were fighting it out in my stomach with no intercessors. And the bed I landed on was not only too short, as all beds are for me, but it resembled a trampoline, springs woven of recycled truck tires cut in strips and a mattress that reminded me of one of my mother's old pot holders. I lay awake trying not to move. Any flex of any muscle reverberated in my stomach like a pebble tossed in a lake. I half expected the sword Excalibur to issue forth and tear into the rest of my guts. I had located a chamber pot in the corner and moved it at the ready near a lump of something that was trying to pass itself off as a pillow.

I did not barf. A ruckus in the hallway took my mind off things. Some drunk was looking for his whore. It seemed that Wally and I had ended up in her usual room.

"Samayanesh!" he called, banging on the door.

I feared he would get in and commit murder when he saw me instead of the woman he wanted. The drunk jabbered. I couldn't understand a word. He pounded on the door. I heard him slide down. I heard him moan.

"Samayanesh," he whined. "Honey, why ain't you in there?"

It was Jack Archibald, and he did know how to pronounce the girl's name.

Next morning, back on the bus with a hangover, Wally Martin gave me his version of Jack Proctor's road.

"It's in the middle of nowhere, going in a nice straight line from nowhere to nowhere," Wally said. "I guess they just wanted to build a road. Maybe some congressman told them to. Since there are so few places that are someplace, all the roads that go from them to someplace else have been built. By Eye-ties. Anyway it works out because after you build a road, no one has any money to take care of it, and if it went from someplace to someplace, people would get upset when it fell apart. This way no one cares."

"Proctor said it was a famine road, to bring food in whenever there was a famine," I said.

"Could be," Wally said. "But Proctor will never get it finished. It floods in there whenever it rains. By the time they get to the end of it, the beginning will have washed away. And by the time they fix the beginning, the end will be gone. It's conceivable that Proctor and his crew could go back and forth building that road forever. Sort of on tenure."

"It doesn't matter that the road has no real purpose?" I asked.

"No one has noticed," he answered.

"Who's paying for it?" I asked.

"The Americans," he said. "And Archibald controls the

purse. Ol' one-eyed jack," Wally said. His red hair was matted and he needed to brush his teeth.

"It *really* doesn't matter that it goes nowhere?" The road was nothing but a castle in the air.

Wally didn't answer. The driver had jammed a cassette into his deck and the tinny speakers shrieked as the hell bus took off, top heavy with baggage, over the flat, bare highlands eaten to desert by goats, sheep, cattle, and the men who were still trying to coax their food from it. The sun was rising, the air was like chilled breakfast wine and the hills that lay behind us were like bones left from a feast.

That night we stayed with Nancy and Bruce Plum, two volunteer teachers, who lived in the town of Adi-Duri, the closest bus stop to both Jiru, where I was headed, and Bari-Cotu, where Wally lived. Bari-Cotu was at the bottom of a hill which had Jiru on the top. It was about five hours on foot from Adi-Duri and Jiru was another hour or so from there. There were no real roads. We walked on a track, sighting on the Jiru hill. Wally insisted I stay at his house so that when it was night, I could look through his scopes at the sky.

Wally had lived in Bari-Cotu for almost four years. He had a little black dog called Cassiopeia because the white spots on her back looked exactly like the constellation. He also had a fortune in telescopes—a lens man. His biggest was mounted on a scaffold that he had built on his roof. His smallest was an antique, in a tooled leather case. Its fittings were brass and silver. It was so finely made, so accurately tuned, that I could use it without my glasses simply by adjusting the series of lenses at both its ends. I held it to my eye and peered over Wally's hedge, hesitating as if I had a premonition. A small brass chain that clipped the telescope to its case was cold on my cheek.

Through it I looked at the village of Bari-Cotu, magnified, a crumble of mud houses and rank alleys. In one bleak doorway someone had planted a red flower, perhaps a geranium, all that would survive there. It struggled with just a stem, its leaves had withered. Time spun backwards, the slender glass in my hand told me how far away that village was, centuries away, millenia. It mocked my coming here, like a visitor from the future. It mocked me as much as the bluff and roar of the one-eyed jacks. When Wally took the glass from my hands, he saw I was weeping and turned in embarrassment to make some tea.

2. Jiru was an unhappy place

Like Bari-Cotu, Jiru was an unhappy place. Its one advantage was the hill. The villagers had built a little house for me, their teacher from a far-off land. It was made of mud and thatch, had a living room, a bedroom, a small place to cook. Out back near the latrine they had rigged a barrel on poles so I could shower—the closest they could come to a white man's house. There was an open veranda that faced north over a shallow valley, divided into tiny farm plots. On the western rim of the valley were shadowy tablelands like the monoliths of ancient civilizations in the distance. At dawn and at sunset their great sides were marked in soft purple tones, strips of earth sometimes as bright as sky.

In Jiru I discovered how, contrary to popular wisdom, poverty is not good for the soul and hardship is not romantic. But I was lulled into not caring much. I used the rich man's defense: the poor don't really suffer as much, the poor can't look for things beyond their simple routines, the poor haven't got much energy.

Sometimes on weekends, I would make the effort and walk to Bari-Cotu and look at stars all night through Wally's scopes. Sometimes we would go to Adi-Duri to supplement our diet of grains and potatoes and see the Plums. But it was rare that I had enough energy to leave my place in Jiru. I didn't even have enough energy to be miserable that, though I had exposed myself to feel what wretches feel, I wasn't sharing any of my superfluity with them. I was just there. My English lessons and my math lessons left a lot to be desired.

My energy level may have been low because I was not eating the diet I had been raised on. There were no peanut butter and olive sandwiches, no hot fudge sundaes, no banana splits, no bacon and eggs in Jiru. There was not much protein in Jiru at the best of times, and though I didn't know it then, we were facing one of the worst of times.

People were making a powder of certain roots and boiling up starchy soups. But it wasn't until about seven or eight months after I got there that I woke up really worried about the food in Jiru. There was less than ever, only a few pounds of potatoes and the odd loaf of bread brought from Adi-Duri by donkey. It had been two weeks since I had seen a carrot, a month since I had tasted a tomato.

Some rains had come. People took their kids out of school and rushed down to their farm plots in the valley where they plowed into a black soil so thick and full of clay that they could only handle it when it was wet. They plowed and seeded from morning 'til night for three straight days and then came back to the village exhausted.

Jiru had a party. Donkey loads of honey were brought in

from the hives for beer. I came shyly from my house that night and stood on the sidelines while Jiru started to dance. I was not shy, however, about taking my share of that honey beer, the sweetness eaten from it as it fermented, a tingling, bitter drink flavored by hops and smoked-out hives. And sooooo good.

Somehow after several big glasses of that wild, raw brew, I got pulled into the circle of dancers. People were calling attention to my fine shoulders claiming that God had made me to do the *iskistis* and nothing else. I was convinced. Personally, I could think of no other reason why God had made my shoulders that way. What a piece of luck that I had come here! What a break! I zuck-zuck-zucked and zick-zick-zicked around that circle like a contestant in a jitterbug marathon. I had never got into the twist, the mashed potato or the bump, even in front of my full length mirror, where I failed miserably at narcissism. But the more Jiru clapped and cheered, the more I revved and clanged those shoulders like pistons in a racing car.

By the end of that party I was famous in Jiru, Bari-Cotu *and* Adi-Duri. I had zicked and zucked those shoulders of mine until my joint bearings seized in their sockets and my motor ran out of gas. That night I made up for years and years of football dances and proms that I'd missed. And I paid for it all the next day too. Dues.

Within a short time the brown valley wore a faint yellow blush and then a fragile green and then gradually a deeper shimmering green as though emerald satin had been thrown over it. But suddenly the rains stopped and the phases of germination and growth repeated themselves in reverse, the fragile green, the yellow blush, the dying brown. As the food dwindled, those who could, including me, walked the three hours to Bari-Cotu to get supplies, and then when those dried up, we went to Adi-Duri, a day to go and a day to come back. I began to see more of Wally Martin and the Plums on these trips.

Wally Martin celebrated the week he discovered his first gray hair. It was absolute proof of maturity and would place him, he said, in the ranks of those who held purses, pulled strings and wore neckties. The Plums walked up from Adi-Duri. We all looked at the hair. Nancy Plum had a bottle of something foul smelling with a handprinted label saying Grecian Formula, which she poured on Wally's head. Bruce Plum searched madly in the mirror for a gray hair of his own but found nothing. We lit a candle to signify the onset of wisdom and we drank three bottles of wine that Wally had been saving for some suitable occasion.

The Plums had just been on a trip to the north. "Things are really bad. I mean *really* bad," Bruce Plum said. "People standing around gas stations begging. We saw a lot of dead animals. It was just bad. I can't describe it."

"It was bad," Nancy Plum agreed. "I mean, I couldn't look at them, those people. Those kids. Just standing there like that. Why aren't they *doing something?*"

"What can they do, Nance?" Bruce asked her.

"I dunno, plant something, I guess."

"It stopped raining," I said.

"Well, I'd do something!" she said.

"What Nance?" Bruce asked her.

"I—I'd get on a bus and go someplace else."

"Nance, they don't have bus fare."

"It's only six tallah," she said.

"*Nance!*" he said. He shook his head at her. "The only people who are getting anything to eat," he went on, "live in Madi-Guri on a bare fucking mountain. Get this, the Americans and Swedes are trying to get these people to plant some trees. The Swedes are hauling in thousands of these tiny seedling pines and the Americans are paying off the villagers in grain rations for the work. They call it Food for Work.

"The mountain was just covered with people scrambling around and planting trees," Nancy Plum said.

"And at the bottom," Bruce went on, "is this fucking big Swede with a pointy little chin and a sextant and this American, a little shit with one eye, pacing back and forth next to piles of wheat and cornmeal."

"Each day after work," Nancy said, "each person who works gets a kilo of wheat and a kilo of corn. Even the kids."

Wally sighed. "I sure wish I could get some of that stuff up here in Bari-Cotu. Get everyone out planting trees and getting some eats on the other end."

"Naw," Bruce Plum said. "They won't agree to that again. Christ, every one of those pissing little trees is going to die unless it rains."

"What about a road, then?" I asked. "A famine road! We'll build a road from Bari-Cotu to Jiru and pay the people with Food for Work."

"What?" Bruce said. "That's a road from fucking nowhere to fucking nowhere."

Nancy said, "Bruce, stop saying fuck all the time."

"So what?" I asked. "I happen to know of another road with similar destinations."

"She's right," Wally Martin said. "And I happen to know that little one-eyed shit."

"Archibald," I said, "of course."

"Let's write to him," Wally said. "All he can say is no."

We wrote:

Dear Mr. Archibald,

It has come to our attention that the townships of Bari-Cotu and Jiru would benefit greatly from the installation of a third-class dirt road. This road, at very low cost, would open up trade and communications between two otherwise isolated communities.

We believe that during this time of dire weather conditions, when farmers are unable to cultivate crops, American Food for Work compensation could make productive use of this labor potential. We also refer to our conversation at the JFK some time ago in which you expressed your views on the expansion of American roadbuilding efforts in the Third World.

We would be willing to plan and supervise the construction of this road under whatever guidelines the United States Agency for International Development requires and look forward to your quick reply.

Sincerely,
Walter W. Martin and
Sarah Easterday

He didn't answer by mail. He came in a helicopter. It circled like a great awkward insect over Bari-Cotu and Jiru, flew churning and chugging down into the ruined valley and ambled back, hovered over Jiru and lowered itself.

Nothing like this had ever happened in Jiru before. I was about to take the opportunity to introduce the new word to my classes—helicopter—but there was no one left in the classroom by the time I got it broken into syllables. Outside, Jack Archibald was leaning out of the machine over a stencilled pair of clasped hands (friendship and cooperation) toward a crowd of kids, tossing hard candies and asking everyone for names which he mispronounced in raucous shouts.

"NO-HANDS?" I heard him yell at Johannus, one of the fifth graders. "Who ever heard of a kid name of NO-HANDS??"

Kids loved it. He looked like a part of that phantasm that had dropped from the sky, a wonderful monster full of sweets and bellowing laughs.

"Say there, No-hands," he hollered, "I'm lookin' for this TAAAAAWL lady." Then he spotted me, clasped Johannus by a shoulder, spun him around and whooped, "Wha, I'll be damned to hell if it ain't MS. SHOULDERS! See that lady over there? She's the one."

He rolled out of the helicopter, appeared to come bouncing along the ground and grabbed me. His pilot, with a desperate gesture, opened a thermos and drank. Steam suggested it was coffee. An empty bottle of Dewar's crashed to the ground in Archibald's wake.

"Now, where in hell do you all want to build this road of yours?"

I pointed down the hill toward Bari-Cotu.

He winked his good eye. "You lookin' for an easy way to get over an' see ol' Wally down there? Do I look like a lil ol' cupid? I got one eye, but I can see as good as any man when it comes to the birds and the bees. But listen honey," he said, "you can't build any roads down that hill. One good rain and it's gonna slide right off." He was laughing so hard he had to prop himself up on three kids who stood by in anticipation of more candy.

"We'll bank it," I told him. I didn't have any idea what I was talking about. "We'll build drains and culverts." The work of rescue, of course, often involves building castles in the air.

"Nope," he answered. "Gals can't build roads. I know, don't bother to say nothing, I'm jest a misuble ol' male chauvinist pig. You may have shoulders like a fullback, but you're still a gal. Yes you are." His arm was around my waist squeezing in easy camaraderie and his boozy breath was wedged like a pocket of smog under my chin.

"But Wally Martin is in on this too," I wheedled.

"Tell you what," he said, his grin as warm as the vapors around him. "You go on and write up a proposal. Tell me how many bags of grain you reckon you need and what you want to do. Be sure and write down how this road of yours is going to move these folks into the twentieth century, cause that's what I'm here for—" he slapped his thigh, "—to move folks right on up to the twentieth century. It ain't easy. No siree."

"Then you'll do it?"

"I ain't saying yes, but I ain't saying no. I'll have to send in a team of my men to see if there's anything to this plan of yours." He went all serious and stuffy. "Jest remember, I got half the U.S. Congress on my back. Wha, I can't tell you to go on and build any ol' goddamn road you like. I'd like to, honey, cross my heart. So you make it a REAL GOOD STORY!"

We could see Wally, his dog Cassiopeia, the heavenly bitch, and half of Bari-Cotu doing double time up the hill toward Jiru.

"Here's comes that ol' copperhead, Wally Martin!" Archibald shouted. "Let's us have a drink on it!"

He pulled a big sack from the helicopter and waved Wally along to the sanctity of my little house, where we ate the picnic, courtesy of the American commissary in the capital—three cans of sardines, one can of deviled ham, a bag of Fritos and a bottle of

Jack Daniel's. Kids from Jiru and Bari-Cotu stared in the windows while we ate and drank. For a split second I felt guilty and then it all seemed so ridiculous: bits of Fritos and the empty tins had fallen to the floor as if the food had dropped, like Archibald himself, from outer space, as if we all had come from another planet. The only consolation, save the taste of those sardines, was that the hungry mouths at my window would not have gone *near* our lunch once they knew it contained pig meat.

Archibald told us how to write the proposal. Something like a shopping list, something like my Uncle Eddie's accounts of the money I'd spent raffling off a Schwinn bicycle for charity when I was ten years old—about twice as much as I'd earned. After he left, Wally and I lost no time. We stayed up all night sipping Jack Daniel's and building a very big castle: The Jiru Road.

3. The JRP changed everyone's life

A letter came from Archibald on official government stationery saying that the Jiru Road Project (JRP, he christened it, suggesting a burp) was being considered for funding. The letter announced the arrival in Bari-Cotu of a team of specialists who would run a feasibility study and investigate the project with regard to its potential effects on the environment, on women, and on population. The letter reeked of after-shave lotion, no doubt applied to cover up for the night before. His signature was huge and traveled grandly across the entire width of the page, ignoring the horizontal and all margins, and ending piled up on itself on the right.

Archibald's team came. Bureaucrats. They did not come in

helicopters like rescuing doves: they came in a Jeep Wagoneer like an invading army. They did not look like people from Goodwill. Even though their Jeep had clasped hands painted on it, I did not believe they had come in friendship and cooperation. We walked with them along the proposed site of the Jiru Road, which Wally and I had gussied up using strips of red cloth from one of my old nightgowns tied to small stakes.

A certain Barbara Clapp ("Dr. Clapp," she insisted,) represented the interests of the Third World Woman. She could not see how the Jiru Road would benefit them "in any real terms," she said, "in the long run." She looked as though she smelled something bad. Wally and I could only think of one real term but it was a short term: it could fill their stomachs and the stomachs of their crying babies for a while.

I told her, "Of course, the road will mean that the women of Jiru and Bari-Cotu can meet, discuss their problems and open up child-care centers. It may lead the way to women in politics."

It's a good thing I have such a silly pug of a nose that I can't look down it at anyone. She never saw my tongue in my cheek. She bit. A turret in my cloud castle.

"I'll have to interview the women," she said.

Charlie Neuter, the environmental protection man, wanted to make sure that the project would not use any DDT and that no endangered species would be threatened by the construction of our road through their habitat. But his main concern was to get out of Jiru before dusk when the malaria mosquitos started biting.

Larry Lewis, the population and rural health investigator, was supposed to find out how the road would effect population growth. Wally told him we could use the road to cart condoms from Bari-Cotu up the hill to Jiru. Fortunately, there was no engineer on Archibald's team, so no one noticed that the road went from nowhere to nowhere and would surely wash away as soon as it rained.

Who knows what that team wrote up in its report? Wally said that in the offices of the food relief establishment, each request for rescue, even as small and insignificant a one as the JRP, gestated in a file where it was nourished on paper—reports, studies, statements and routine correspondence. We made several trips to the capital to defend our idea, until nine months later the JRP, our baby, was born. And not any too soon for there still had been no rain, and the shadowy mesas across the valley from my veranda were moving in closer and closer as though the world were shrinking, drying, shriveling like a fruit in the sun.

The people of Jiru were drying out as well. Kids came to school, but they couldn't learn. They sat and looked at me or out the window with an expression I knew too well, one I had seen many times in the pictures of Krosinski's *Great American Disasters,* one I had seen on my own mother's face once. I remembered it now as clearly as if I were locked against her chest on that pitched and rocking raft in which we had ridden out the great Kansas flood of 1951—the weak surprise, the tired surrender of real fear. But a drought is not like a flood. It devastates slowly, like cancer, with a daily hope that a cure will be found, or a magic healing will take place. It's easy enough to ignore the discomfort until the symptoms rage.

I felt that my relationship with the people of Jiru had always been distant. Does it make any sense to say that it was precisely this distance that brought us together? Those kids, sitting formally at their desks each day, though not so bright-eyed as before, were putting out for me the last whispers of their energy.

So I, despite my nonstop low blood sugar headaches, put out for them. I didn't know how long I could go on. By the time the first trucks full of Food for Work arrived in Bari-Cotu there were just three loaves of stale bread and a ten pound sack of sorghum left in Jiru.

Jack Archibald came, just above the trucks, making as much noise as his helicopter, scattering hard candies like hail and hollering "HOWDY DOWN THERE!" as his pilot lowered him into the crowd of gathering road builders.

The entire population of both towns turned out. Musicians, long silent, dragged out their instruments, thumb pianos, drums, harps, kept time somehow with Archibald, who catapulted into them singing something that sounded like "The Battle Hymn of the Republic."

"Put yer faaaaahn crystal in a safe place, this ol' Jack is about to BER-REAK GLASS!"

Jack Archibald's pilot finished one thermos and opened another. If he had coffee in them, it didn't do much good because he fell sound asleep sitting up just as Archibald, looking for all the world like Santa Claus in a red Windbreaker, threw his International Harvester cap into the air and waved some money around, offering it to whoever could catch his cap.

No one understood a word he said. They watched the hat take wing, soar on a puff of wind and fall, bright as the flowers that would bloom in their valley if only the rains would come. Little Johannus, who felt less dismay than the rest of us, picked up the cap and put it on at a jaunty angle and ran to the fat man who dropped candy whenever he appeared from the sky.

"Well I'll be damned to hell!" ol' Jack roared. "If it ain't ol' NO-HANDS! Say, I remember this lil tyke," he said. "Growin' like a weed. Jest about as big as ol' Jack. Jest like a weed." He held the boy aloft then, all bones and bright scabs (without food, sores don't heal) suspended in the air, high on his loud bluff.

Then within a few seconds Wally and I were in his clutch. He handed us a carton of what shook around like Fritos.

"Well now," he said. "I LIKE what you kids are doing out here. I like it."

He folded his arms over his belly, head tipped to one side, mouth in a pout and his good eye winking madly with a tic under the thick lens. "Never you mind what ol' Barbara's Clap had to say. Wha, she ain't interested in wimmin," tumbling into Wally with an elbow in the ribs. "I'll send that gal out this way and she'll show you about how wimmin are developed!

"And Larry Lewis," he hooted, this time knocking me in the kidneys with a slap, "turns out the oney thing he ever knew about population control was that he couldn't get his up! NEVER COULD!!!"

And then he was gone. He shook his pilot back to life, poured some hooch down his throat and they gurgled skyward.

By now everyone had peeked into the sacks that were coming down from the trucks. A few of the women were sifting yellow cornmeal through their fingers and looking glum.

"They don't eat cornmeal," Wally whispered. "I bet they don't even know what it is."

There was a funny hush then. Everyone stared at the sacks—Gift of the American People, a flag, the clasped hands. I felt the tension: they knew they would have to eat something they didn't trust, something that wasn't their food, something that other people from another country didn't want.

The JRP changed everyone's life. There was energy in the morning, and though it did not feel as though we had been rescued, we had forestalled disaster. There was hope. There was even something to do. From Bari-Cotu to the bottom of the Jiru Hill was only a short distance, flat and rock strewn. No grass was left on it and its soil had blown away a few months ago. There were dead bushes which now and then would produce a flower or two, small and bright yellow, brighter than normal everyone said, almost orange. You could see those flowers for miles as if they were calling out desperately for bees. But all the bees in Jiru were gone. The hives that produced the honey for the famous Jiru beer were empty, hung like buckets in the bare trees as though an alcoholic giant had gone on a bender.

All that was left between the two towns were the rocks and all we had to do on the flat to build our road was move them out of the way and then level the track.

Everyone worked on the road. Men put rocks into baskets and hauled them off to the side. Kids sorted through them and arranged them according to size and shape. Women laid the flat stones along the edges of the road like guard rails and when we had to pass over a low spot they filled it with small stones and earth so it wouldn't wash away. Going up was harder. The hill had been eroding for centuries. It was pocked and pitted, ditched and channeled. We had to install culverts, build banks and grade curves. Our road was like a work of art. Each afternoon we all stood around and admired it.

It was hard not to take the road seriously, even though it went from nowhere to nowhere. In the evenings, Wally and I and whoever else was around would walk its length. Wally began to dream up another road, one that would connect Bari-Cotu with Adi-Duri, thereby linking it, Wally insisted, to Rome.

We were sitting on top of a gully picking twigs from a dead bush and tossing them here and there at will. Cassiopeia, Wally's celestial bitch, chased the twigs. We figured out what we would have to tell the team of Neuter, Clapp and Lewis. It was dark and Wally pulled a small telescope from his rucksack and shot a quick peek at the sky.

"I've been photographing Crux every night to chart its progress," he said. "I gotta get home fast to catch it at zenith."

And I watched him go with Cassiopeia twinkling at his heels. He was thinner now than when we first met. We all were. And his red hair had lost some of its light, but it still seemed like a beacon as he bounced down that hill.

Once the whole area surrounding our villages had been grazing land. But there were no cattle left, not even in Adi-Duri. The farmers had sold off all their livestock as the rains refused to come: starved cattle, worth next to nothing. A few goats still wandered around, nearly wild, worse than useless because they were eating the bark from the scrub and the dry roots of the grass. When the rains came there would be no grass left to spring to life.

I could smell a goat nearby, hear it rustling in the brush behind me. I lifted to my knees and peered down into the gully.

The goat was tied. Someone must have been feeding it Food for Work grain because unlike the other goats, it had flesh and its udder was full of milk.

Then I heard someone coming toward the goat, softly padding bare feet and then a face blanched by moonlight.

It was Alganesh, the most beautiful girl in Jiru. Her marriage had taken place three months ago and she was pregnant now. She gave the goat some cornmeal and knelt behind it in the dust. Milked it into a small bowl and drank and milked and drank again.

I realized suddenly that she was the only pregnant woman in Jiru. There had been so many miscarriages that people began to suspect witchcraft, not malnutrition. Women who had come to full term were having stillborns. This was not going to happen to Alganesh. She finished her meal, covered her head with her thin white veil and moved like mist back to the village.

4. It was on the morning of the gathering clouds

Wally got a message that Nancy Plum was pregnant and that they had decided to leave Adi-Duri, so we went down to say goodbye. Cassiopeia followed cleverly and quietly at a distance until she knew we had passed the point of no return and she would get to come along. Suddenly she appeared, chased ahead of us, shadow-barking, as though we had known she was there all along.

"I thought so," Wally said. There was nothing he could do about it. Cassie, he said, hated to stay home alone.

The Plums had cooked up all their remaining food. An oddball feast. There was enough peanut butter for seven crackers. There were three tins of K-ration beef stew spiked with four dried chillies and plopped on top of a few boiled noodles, extended by a few mashed potatoes. There was Food for Work corn bread. Nancy had dug up a prehistoric cabbage and some carrot shards at the market and made a salad. Oh, where were the salads of yesteryear?

"If it's a little girl," Bruce Plum said, "We're calling her Grace. Because she's *amazing!* Nance was on the pill."

"Maybe they were stale," Nancy suggested.

We sat around picking our teeth and talking about how strange it would be to go home to stuffed supermarkets and four lane highways.

"Not me," Wally said. "I never want to go back there."

"But it's getting so bad here," Nancy said. "I mean I just can't deal with it. Like when there's a famine, isn't the UN supposed to do something about it?"

"I dunno," Wally said. "Maybe they don't know."

"Fuck that," Bruce said. "They know."

We had seen it along the main road in Adi-Duri. The nomads had come up from the great deserts that spread east toward the Red Sea. They were begging on the streets and moving south to beg in the towns on the road to the capital. And they were people who would rather steal than beg. It was as though they had no strength left, even to rob. They were camping in the dry stream beds with their camels. Bruce Plum said that their cattle were dead, heaped along the escarpment road—never made it to the market. Wally and I clucked in sympathy, but we were like chickens standing safely in the eye of a storm. Every month those friendly and cooperative trucks pulled into Bari-Cotu full of grain. Of course, we also knew that storms float in the atmosphere and there was no telling how long we could hold that calm center.

There was a whine and a scratch at the door and Cassiopeia appeared. She had been hit by a car or a truck and had come dragging herself by her front legs. Her back seemed to be broken and we figured there must have been internal injuries because there was blood at her mouth.

There was, of course, no vet in Adi-Duri. There wasn't even a people doctor. Bruce Plum offered gallantly to put her to sleep.

Wally refused, wanting to wait until morning to see how she was.

By morning the bleeding had stopped. She drank some water. It was revealed that only one leg had been broken. Wally claimed that a three-legged dog was not so improbable, so we carried her back home, wrapped in an old Plum blanket, to Bari-Cotu. For a few days the dog rose and sank. Sometimes she seemed to improve and then she got worse. The problem was a fever which Wally attributed to an infection. He gave her some penicillin and the fever went down. Then it went up again. At one point, in something like a delirium, she bit Wally on the wrist. Just a nip.

The people of Bari-Cotu and Jiru did not like dogs. Who could blame them? There was rabies all over the place. But there were some people, mostly school children, who couldn't resist Cassie, especially after we had started to build the road. She was comic relief, a clown. She carried rocks, played hide-and-seek.

During her last few days Wally brought her in a basket to the road work so he could watch her and feed her small drops of meal mixed with water. She looked like night in her basket, the white spots of the constellation on her side.

One day a little gourd full of goat's milk appeared next to her. She sniffed eagerly at it, rallied, lapped it with excitement from Wally's palm.

"Where did this come from?" Wally asked.

I told him, "Alganesh has a secret goat."

That goat milk was Cassie's last meal.

It was on the morning of the gathering clouds. I fetched my camera to mark the event. I still have the pictures. Wally came to

Jiru looking for some chloroquine. He had a fever and a terrible headache.

"Malaria," he said.

He had taken the first course of four tablets and had run out. He didn't feel so bad, he said. And the sight of those clouds and the promise of rain was making him feel better every minute.

I took pictures of Wally against the background of the clouds. He took pictures of me against them. I took pictures of my students, of their parents, of anyone who wandered in front of my shutter.

The clouds were piled on the mesas like feather beds. They were dancing in the high heavens, wisps of cirrus like lover's vows. They were thickening toward the north like butter in a churn.

Oh God! It was glorious. We called off our road work. We stood in awe. We all believed.

Wally stayed in Jiru that night. His headache was so bad, he couldn't walk back to Bari-Cotu. He was beginning to feel pain at the top of his spine. We waited for the chloroquine to start working. "Sometimes, if it's bad," he said, "it takes awhile."

I heard him tossing on my couch and then, finally, he quieted, went to sleep. He woke up late the next morning not well, but not worse.

"The clouds are gone," he said softly.

I was on the veranda looking at the bare mesas, angry red in the morning light.

He drank some tea, but he couldn't eat. His fever was high. Neither of us had a thermometer, but heat was coming off him in BTU's.

"You know what's weird," he said. "The fever doesn't crack.

Whenever I've had malaria before, the fever cracked. Maybe it hasn't gone high enough yet."

He went back to bed. This time in my room.

By midmorning he still wasn't able to get up. I made him some more tea. He looked terrible.

"What if it's cerebral?" I asked. The malaria we had all heard of, the one that likes to eat the blood cells in your brain, the one that the chloroquine won't touch. "Why don't I walk down to Adi-Duri. I can call the Peace Corps."

I had a funny feeling then, a premonition, about rescue being very far away. It was six hours to that phone in Adi-Duri. I couldn't even be back that night.

"Naw," he answered. "You don't need to call them. Just pick up some primaquine: I've used that when the chloroquine fails."

I walked fast to Adi-Duri, alone, striding out the full length of my long legs. I don't remember that walk at all. I went straight to call the Peace Corps before the office closed. There was only one phone in the town, installed during the Second World War. It stood enshrined in a red closet at the far end of the post office, where its wires met in a confused fray. It suffered constant repairs. Even while I was trying to call the Peace Corps, the man whose sole job it was to keep that phone alive had to go inside its mouthpiece and do something. He pulled some wires with his teeth, and returned it to me with an uncertain grin. He looked as though he had also been installed during the Second World War.

To no avail. The phone shot a blast of static into my ear. Then my words went into it and reverberated along the wires as though I had twanged them. Nothing.

We tried again. This time we got the operator in the capital. I gave her the number. I thought I could hear Margie Stout, the Peace Corps nurse, on the other end. I screamed, *"Margie! Margie is that you? This is Sarah Easterday from Jiru."*

All I could hear was a faint and muffled "Who?"

"Sarah from Jiru. Jiru. Can you hear me?"

There was a muffled ringing and another voice was on, clear as a bell, speaking German and then, an answering voice, another German.

"I've crossed lines," I told the telephone man.

He listened to the Germans a few minutes. Hung up and yanked at some of the wires that dangled under the phone.

We tried again. This time I could hear Margie, "Hello, Peace Corps medical office." But she couldn't hear me.

"Margie Margie!" I yelled against her string of hellos.

"These damn phones," she finally muttered and hung up.

"Don't hang up," I called. I heard my plea fade along the wires.

We tried again and again and it rang, but each time Margie picked up the receiver, we were cut off, or we cut into the Germans again. I envied them their conversation.

"Wie gehts?" I called into the phone on the off chance they might hear me and be able to get a message to Margie. *"Wie gehts?* Can you hear me?" But they were on a wire all their own. At last even their voices grew fainter and fainter and the Adi-Duri connection sputtered like an old engine and died.

"Come back tomorrow," the old man said. "Sometimes it can be better in the morning."

I went to the chemist's shop and bought Wally some primaquine. I went to the coffeehouse where I took a room. They had some eggs, they told me. If I would like, they could cook me some eggs for supper. But I was too worried about Wally to eat, even an egg. I was too worried about Wally to go to bed. I ordered some tea, then sat under their single fluorescent light wondering what to do.

There were three men at the table next to mine. I heard them say that they were driving back to the capital the next day. I was facing one of them over my tea. He was staring at me, so I stared back.

Finally he asked, "Do you live here? Are you a Peace Corps?"

"Yes," I answered, "I live in Jiru."

He was wearing an outrageous tie, wide as his skinny chest. My eyes were so bad that I couldn't make out the designs, but I hallucinated, saw something that looked like a great cauliflower.

"You must be teaching English?" he asked.

"Yes," I answered.

The others turned toward our conversation, looked me over and turned away.

"And you?" I dared to ask. I thought that people in such ties might not like prying questions. So I quickly added, "The reason I'm asking is that I need some help."

"Help?" he said.

"Yes, I have a friend who is very sick and we want to send a message to the Peace Corps. The phone here is temporarily out of order. And the mail is a little slow. So perhaps you could be so kind, *if* you are going to the capital tomorrow (I didn't want to let on that I had heard their conversation) . . ."

"What is wrong with your friend?"

The others were now interested: they all turned to look at me.

"Malaria," I told them. "But the medicine isn't working. We think it might be a resistant strain."

"Perhaps." The man shifted slightly in his seat. His tie twisted, revealing a deep green border dotted with purple like clusters of grapes. "Sadly, you people do not seem to have strength against such diseases."

I nodded.

"We would be most happy to assist you in your trouble," the man closest to me said.

His back had been toward me. Now I could see his face. He was young, fine boned, with the high domed forehead of the highland aristocracy. They all nodded in agreement.

"Americans are our friends," the small one on the left said.

Did he mean it?

"Thank you," I answered. "I hope we may continue to deserve your friendship."

I was keeping it formal. With travelers wearing suits and ties, you never knew who might be who. "It's a great good fortune we have met," I went on in the high mode, "because I was worrying and wondering how to solve my problem. Have you been traveling long?"

"Three weeks only," my friend in the fruited tie answered. "We are from the Ministry of the Interior and we have been inspecting certain wildlifes. As you may know, this area contains large concentrations of bleeding heart baboons. We are estimating their populations for the World Wildlife Society in case they are becoming extinct."

Bleeding heart baboons. The terror of the Jiru valley. A troop of them had come into the village one night to raid the grain stores. I heard the commotion, saw lanterns and flaming torches. I pitched right into the fray, ran down the hill with my light into a storm of flying rocks and shrieks. The baboons were screaming, weird yells and barks, almost human. They looked like humans too, all arms, legs and mouths, caught and confused. They hurled stones back with frightening accuracy, but soon they were outnumbered, outshouted, outpelleted, and they began to run away. The largest male turned to face the crowd as his harem and children beat their retreat. On his chest was a hard shining platelike shield. It arched, bright as red paint. Vicious, he stood with his sharp teeth bared, his great mane like a lion's ruffed with anger; his chest gleamed in our lights.

"Tell me, are the baboons feeling the effects of this drought?" I asked them.

"That is what we are checking up about," the small one said.

"And the people?" I dared to ask it. I *had* to ask it. "We are seeing problems in Jiru," I added.

"Periodically we suffer from drought," the tie said. "We are used to it."

"Yes, I suppose that's true."

"You have no droughts in America?" the small one asked.

"We do," I answered.

"So you see," the aristocrat said. "You see the problem."

"When there is a drought in one part of my country," I told him, "we send help from another part where there is no drought. Like that."

"Even we do this," the tie said. Perhaps he resented my tone: he seemed miffed. His tie rose on his chest. I thought I saw a bunch of carrots where it knotted.

"So do we," the small one chimed.

"Well, I have been wondering," I said, "when some help will come here. There has been no rain for almost three years." There was silence.

The aristocrat smiled. "But surely by now you have noticed," he said, "this is *not your* country."

It was meant to shut me up and it did.

"About this message," the tie said. "Perhaps you will write it now. We leave very early in the morning."

I wrote:

> Margie,
>
> Please come right away. Wally Martin has malaria and the chloroquine is not working. I cannot reach you by phone. Wally is at my house in Jiru.
>
> Sarah Easterday

I folded the paper and handed it to the aristocrat who was holding out his hand. He had the most beautiful face I had ever seen.

"I hope your friend will be well soon," he said. "And I, personally, will deliver this letter for you."

There were clouds again the next morning, tall pillars of them like monuments in the sky. I hoped, as I walked back to Jiru, that when I got there I would see Wally on my veranda, past the crisis, looking at the cosmos through one of his scopes, watching it fill with the promise of rain. But wishing only makes it so if you happen to be Cinderella. The clouds blew away before I got to Jiru and Wally was not on the veranda. I could hear him moaning from somewhere deep in my tiny house, an awful rattling moan like a hound spooked by the moon.

My door was open and I looked past it into a room that had been torn to shreds. Cushions and clothes were strewn everywhere. The table was tipped, its contents a rubble on the floor.

"Wally! Wally!" I called. I suspected a robbery.

I heard him from my bedroom, "I'm sorry."

He was on the bed, sitting with his back against the wall. His eyes were yellow, and the sheets tossed all around him, a testimony to his suffering. "The pain," he said, "is making me mad. I've taken fourteen aspirins. I think it's helping." He tried to smile.

"I've got the primaquine." I ran to him as he toppled, caught him before he fell from the bed.

"Oh Jesus, I'm weak as shit," he whispered. His hands were shaking.

I had never seen anyone so sick.

He took the primaquine.

That night I heard him sobbing. I went in there.

"It won't stop," he whined. "The fever won't break. Flames. A lake of flames." He pointed toward the door. "There. The flames."

He was hallucinating.

For a moment I felt panic. Wanted to run away from him, leave him. I knew there was nothing I could do. It flashed through my mind that I had been a fool to trust those men from the Ministry of the Interior. I saw them tossing my letter out the window of their car and laughing at me. I saw that aristocrat's face, beautiful, remote, as he found the letter in his pocket three days later, slightly embarrassed because he had forgotten. I saw him crumple it and throw it away. I believed we had been abandoned. I stood staring at Wally.

"Fire," he cried. "Get me out of here."

The bed was drenched with his sweat; he smelled like flowers fermenting, left too long in a vase.

I soaked rags in cool water and laid them on his head, in his arm pits, on his inner thighs, and as I did this I felt myself grow dull to his agony. The room seemed like a glossy print. I accepted what was happening as though I'd turned a page in the Krozinski book of disasters and seen a photograph of something wild and unexpected, something huge that had been shrunk to the confines of a page, the terror of its moment stilled.

Wally quieted. I went outside. On the veranda I found one of his telescopes: he never traveled without one. I looked through it (for a sign?) but it hadn't been positioned on the stars, and all I saw was the rim of the earth and the huge black tablelands, ominous, magnified two thousand times, like walls closed around us. I spun away from the glass.

"Is he getting well?" It was Alganesh, carrying a gourd of milk, very pregnant, so shy, wrapped in white like an angel, trying to help.

Oh, how I understood what she was doing. I collapsed in tears, a great bony heap, awkward even in my weeping.

She touched my shoulders which heaved in despair. "God will help him," she said. "This milk is for you."

I boiled the milk with tea leaves. I added a lot of sugar. I drank it. It was sweet and delicious. It tasted of goat and grass and the dust and smoke of Alganesh's gourd. I realized it had been almost two days since I had eaten. The taste of that rich tea made me forget Wally. I forgot everything. I was a mouth and a stomach, and I was blood which had been crying for nourishment.

Toward morning I heard Wally stir, but when I looked in on him he was still sleeping. I felt him. He burned. The cloths which I had used to cool him were dried, stiff with his sweat and sloughed about the bed. I gathered them up, rinsed them, and soaked them again. I lay one carefully on his forehead.

He opened his eyes, reached for my hand and howled, hurling the wet cloth away from him.

"Ai-aaaaaaaaaah!" He screamed, waved his hands in front of his face. "Get it away from me. Get away! Away! That cloth!" He cringed, shivering, out of control.

"Wally?" I said. I wanted to say, Wally, where are you? I felt in my bones that he was gone. A monster was left in his place. His jaw was slack. Spit drooled from it. He fell back into the bedclothes. He seemed to fall apart. Again I went to wipe him with a cool rag, again he attacked.

"No! No! No! No! No!" he shouted, shaking his head back and forth in agony.

"Oh Wally . . ."

I backed away, ran into my living room, and like a mad woman, tried to pick up the mess. The cushions defied me: I didn't know where to put them. I wandered around with a book looking for the bookcase. I swept at broken glass with my hand. You are frantic, I told myself. Be calm, help *must* be on the way.

It was. I heard the whirr of it, the churning song of rescue. Noah's dove, Archibald's helicopter lowering itself into the middle of Jiru. I ran to it. Its propellers were beating out "It's O.K., it's O.K., it's O.K., O.K., O.K.," like train wheels knocking toward home.

"Where's the sick kid?" the pilot asked. "I'm supposed to be picking up some sick kid," he said.

"Yes, yes," I told him. "We need help. He can't walk." He went for Wally. Into the rubble of my house walked the pilot and three men from town.

"He's delirious," I told the pilot. "He's had a fever too long. He's hallucinating. There."

We looked in at Wally. He was sitting, pressed stiff against the wall, his knees rolled up against his chin, staring. His eyes were sunk deep into his head, his breath rasped from a dry throat, his lips swollen and cracked.

"Let me give him some water," I said. "He's so dry."

I came toward him with a glass of water held in my two hands like an offering, a prayer. "Wally," I whispered. "Just drink this, O.K.?"

He roared, lunged at me from the bed, knocked the water from my hands and fell forward, exhausted, his head rolling; his arms like pendulums swung a few times against the floor.

"Jesus," the pilot said.

They tied Wally to keep him in the plane. I didn't think it was necessary: he was done by then, spent. The last I saw of him was his shock of wild red hair against the window as they closed the helicopter. My heart surged with that awkward tadpole of a machine as it sang up into the air, "Yes-O.K., yes-O.K., yes-O.K." I waved and waved until I couldn't see them anymore. I waved a long time.

Little Johannus was standing behind me. "Where is that great Lord with the sweets?" he asked. "The one who lives in the belly of that big insect?"

The next week a letter came.

> Dear Sarah,
>
> Wally does not appear to have malaria. We have evacuated him to the American army hospital in Frankfurt, Germany, where his case can be evaluated. We suspect encephalitis. We will let you know as

soon as we have word. We know you must be terribly worried.

Sincerely,
Margery Stout
RN, USPC

I have kept all the letters Margie sent me. They are like the unraveling of my premonition, the last pieces in the puzzle of foreshadowings.

Dear Sarah,

Wally is in a coma. They are quite sure that it is encephalitis. They can only treat the symptoms at this time and hope for the best. I will write again as soon as there is more news. He is in good hands.

Margie

Dear Sarah,

Wally Martin has died. We are all so shocked. I hope you will understand Peace Corp's request that you take care of Wally's things. Close his house and return whatever valuables you find to us, so that we may forward them to his parents. We leave it to you, since you are the only one there.

The director says that you must feel free to take some leave and return to the capital to be with friends. I know you and Wally were close and this will be a hard time for you.

They are investigating the cause of death in Germany. I will let you know immediately if you need to take any precautions.

With sympathy,
Margie

Dear Sarah,

The hospital in Frankfurt reports that Wally Martin died of rabies. An autopsy revealed the virus in his brain. There was evidence of a bite on his wrist. We are alarmed that Wally did not take the bite seriously and report for the Pasteur treatment. Please be alerted to the dangers of this disease.

If you had any contact with Wally's saliva, come at once to the capital.

Yours,
Margie

Cassiopeia. Dead before we knew what she had. What a bitter, sinking feeling I had as that sad irony filled my heart.

There was also a letter from Archibald:

Dear Sal,

I surely won't blame you if you up and leave that road on us. But don't worry, we can figure out a way to keep that old cornmeal coming. Nobody's going to think you left because of being a gal either. That ol' copperhead Wally was my kind of kid.

Jack Archibald

The whole thing was written in his big scrawl, like waves on a stormy sea. I wrote back to tell him that I had no intention of leaving Jiru.

The hardest part was closing Wally's house. More than once I wept. Sobs that came in waves and had half of Bari-Cotu peering in the windows and doors. I couldn't get the sight of him from my mind, that viral madness, terrified of water. And now he was gone, I'd never see him again, he'd never see the road finished, never see that rain when it finally came.

I sputtered and heaved and dribbled as I gathered his things. My choked breaths were wracking, my whines loud. In Wally's pitted bedroom mirror my face was unrecognizable, the eyes puffed and red under those thick foggy lenses, my nose aflame, my lips thin slivers almost gone, drained of all their color by my sorrow. Oh, pull yourself together, Shoulders, I told that horrible image. You don't have a face for grief. It's bad enough as it is. But instead I fell apart, wailed and howled like the whole lost tribe of Israel.

I gave Wally's clothes and furniture to his special friends in Bari-Cotu. I saved two blankets for Alganesh's baby, who came into the world, as if obeying some primordial law, just as Wally left it. I packed his maps of the heavens, his sequence of the passage of Crux, enlarged, mounted on his living room wall, a constant view of the night sky. I packed his souvenirs, the baskets, the embroidered cloths, the nomad knives he had collected over the past years. At last I packed his telescopes. There were twenty-two. All sizes, all kinds. But just before I sealed up the box, I removed the little antique with the silver trim, my favorite, the one I had first looked through, down into Bari-Cotu. I wanted to keep it. So I put a note in the box explaining my intrusion, my borrowing, my theft, to his parents, and I told them what Wally and I had been up to on that road and about how I meant to finish it for him.

I held the little scope to my eye, so finely made, so accurately tuned. I peered over Wally's hedge. The small brass chain that held the instrument in its case was cold on my cheek. Bari-Cotu was still there. I had thought, perhaps, there was a remote chance that it had disappeared along with Wally Martin. But it was still crumbled in its rank, sad alleys, the same except that the red flower, the geranium I had seen that first day, was gone. That village still mocked my coming and now Wally's going, and for a few moments I wanted to leave as well because I knew that nothing was going to change there for a long, long time.

No one in the capital could understand why I stayed on in Jiru after Wally died.

"You are the only volunteer in the district," the office wrote. "The director has agreed that should you like to change situation, we will do everything in our power to assist."

A lot of volunteers had been leaving the northern villages because they couldn't get enough to eat. The medical office circulated a memo:

> Re: Malnutrition.
>
> We have been seeing too many cases of malnutrition among volunteers. Do not remain in a remote posting if you are not able to procure an adequate diet. You are no good to anyone if you become sick.
>
> Margery Stout

Of course, I had the Food for Work and a bottle of megavitamins which I had been sharing with Alganesh. Sometimes Archibald would send a "Care package" along with the cornmeal, rice and powdered milk. But I had lost my taste for Fritos, Cheddar Cheese Puffs and Milk Duds. Their bright crackling cellophanes ridiculed our bare bread and rice. I felt as I looked at those crisp dazzling packages that something was wrong in God's grand design.

I must admit, however, that I did partake of the liquids that came in those Care packages. In the brief twilight that flutters along the equator, I toasted our daily progress on the road and worried about the day it would finish because we still needed that food. I could see that road inching its way up our hill. The two culverts were in. I had hoped it might disintegrate like Jack Proctor's road, and we could start at the ruined beginning, go back and forth between Bari-Cotu and Jiru until the rains came.

Sometimes I went on toasting until well after twilight because there was no one to warn me about people who drink alone. At those times I would feel alone in the universe, in an African night as black as blindness and I would wish for the sounds of traffic. I would wish for the lights of neighbors. And sometimes, the village of Jiru, trying to sleep even though it was just too early to go to bed, would be kept awake by the strange sounds of their long and mellow teacher, a pale shadow of Ella Fitzgerald, singing "My Funny Valentine" like a hound baying at the moon, a song which seemed appropriate when I longed for love. And a song which I felt I could open up and sing because I knew the folks below couldn't understand a word.

Usually there was nothing to do in Jiru after dark.

5. I didn't know enough about home brew to be afraid

Well, I was not the only one in Jiru to get my hands on some hooch. It didn't take long for an enterprising wag named Afewerk to start brewing a white lightning called *araki* from the Food for Work corn. One night I was attracted by the sound of a drum from the far side of the village. It wasn't really a party at that point. Afewerk was selling glasses of *araki* at his front door and everyone was sitting there quietly tying one on. The drum was being thumped casually by Afewerk's brother, Tesfa, as a sort of advertising.

I didn't know enough about home brew to be afraid, so when the villagers, edging me along, insisted I try a glass, I went ahead. That *araki* was the strongest stuff I ever felt zoom by my tonsils. It had no taste and by the time it reached my throat, it had vaporized and made right for my lungs where it did its business directly with the blood stream, completely by-passing the stomach.

It was a cold night and in a wild mood of let's-throw-it-out-the-window, these normally staid and cautious folk, who had seen the last of their trees forty or fifty years ago, decided to build a bonfire. Everyone rushed around dredging up scraps of old rags and bits of wood. We couldn't spare it, but we spared it, and the fire roared up against all reason and sense, against the drab hungry round of our lives, against the loss of rain and good food, against the losses at birth, against the escalation of death, against the encroaching shadows of those distant mesas as the air thinned and dried and space and time was consumed.

I knew (I had only had two *arakis* by then) that we would all lament the waste of wood in the morning, but that fire made my heart sing and that *araki* froze my brain, and when those drums sounded (not just for advertising this time) my legs were already dancing and my shoulders, a living legend in Jiru, jumped to the *iskistis* with such abandon that my ribs knocked like wind chimes in a hurricane.

All of Jiru cheered me into the middle of a circle, shoulders all around pumped and crashed. Voices all around zuck-zuck-

zucked. A high, nasal female voice started the song of the young bride and the old husband who couldn't. Tesfa came along and locked me with his stare, zucking his shoulders as close to mine as he could without knocking into me. I zucked away. Everyone laughed. He zuck-zucked after me, driving his shoulders like pistons, bent his knees and walked hunkering. His zucks were almost hisses, a low whining sound brought them forth. I gave in, zucked forward, bent my knees and arched my neck in his direction. He pulled, zucking, away and then moved in. On the springs of his snapping shoulders, his arms, palms up, were supple as new green branches.

I was afraid I looked like a half-starved, pecked-at chicken, my arms flapped like broken wings, but with three *arakis* in me, I didn't care. Besides, something told me that this *iskistis* going on right now was about as close as I was going to get to courtship.

Children who had never seen anything like it peered through the bowed and thumping legs of the circle, a few, risking the trample, rushed in zucking and yelling.

People were starting to vomit and pass out when there was a shout that baboons had come, were into the stores, devouring the Food for Work, gift of the American People, without having done a single thing for it.

The circling dancers broke, rushing in all directions, forgetting where they were. I staggered after Tesfa as if we had just married, fell, scraped my knees and lost my glasses.

I was feeling my way along the ground as the crowd passed over me like a leapfrog marathon. I knew there was no chance for those glasses to have survived, but when the rush was over, I opened my eyes. All I could see was a red glow from the dying bonfire, a light which fortuitously caught a sparkle on the ground.

I groped along toward it on all fours.

My glasses! One of the lenses was still alive.

I tried them on to figure out where I was. I was drunk. I was teetering. I felt I was on the verge of the world itself, the peak, Mt. Ararat. Below and all around me with no direction, I heard the noises of battle, shouting humans and barking, shrieking baboons.

Like a victim of blindman's buff, I turned around and around trying to get my bearings, when I saw something skulk past me. There were three or four of them, sunk low, heads down. They looked like hyenas, but they were men. And they had a girl in the grass. I heard her screaming.

There was no help, no rescue save what I could give her, so I stumbled furiously in the direction of that call, hurled myself into what looked like a dog fight and started socking. The last thing I remember was the crack of a wooden club against my skull.

What happened between then and the time I found myself standing half in and half out of the Day-Glo pink interior of the John F. Kennedy Memorial Coffee House and Bar in Makele, I'll never really know. I was told later that Tesfa and Afewerk found me next morning in their house and dragged me, bonked and blinded, to my own house, so they claimed, where I had gone peacefully to sleep. I must have woken well before dawn of the following day, donned another pair of glasses and headed for the bus in Adi-Duri.

I hadn't washed, brushed my teeth or changed my clothes. No wonder as I walked into the JFK a path opened in front of me. The event that brought me back to reality, however, was a high, loud whoop as of a rare flightless bird: "WELL, I'LL BE DAMNED TO HELL!!"

From grainy pink shadows, I saw the form of a short, fat man emerge, pattern of dots, lights and darks, reds and purples, like a pointillist painting coming into focus. It was, of course, Jack Archibald, looking like a sawed-off Roy Rogers in a deep violet cowboy suit and a pure white Stetson.

"What in blue Jesus happened to you, gal?" he asked. "Wha, if you didn't already start out lookin' like you'd been smashed by a truck, I'd hafta say, Hey, YOU BEEN SMASHED BY A TRUCK???"

"Oh God," I moaned. I reached up into my hair and felt a muck. What was it? It felt like a dried paint rag.

"Am I O.K.?" I was hoping that he knew.

"Honey, you smell jest like my Aunt Lucy," he told me. "All's you need is some hair of the dog, a little fire to fight fire."

He materialized a gallon of Cutty Sark, like a magician pulling a rabbit from a hat.

I moaned.

"SAMAYANESH!" he bellowed. "Samayanesh, sugar, bring around some of them cold beers you been saving for me."

And before I knew what was happening, two of Archibald's boilermakers were winging their way toward my ruined bones. My shoulders felt as though they had come unhinged, dropped to the ground and been put back together by someone who forgot most of the important pieces. I was sure that someone had been shaking my head so hard that my eyeballs had exchanged places.

"There was a party in Jiru last night," I told Archibald.

"Well I guess to hell," he said.

Though he had splashed on gallons of after-shave, I could tell there had been a party someplace else last night too.

"Two nights ago," I corrected. "They made this stuff called . . ."

"*ARAKI!*" he yowled. He snatched my boilermaker from me.

"Honey," he said, "You wasn't drunk, you was poisoned.

"*ARAKI?*" he repeated. "You drank that shit?"

It started to come back. The *iskistis,* the baboons, the girl in trouble, the whack on my head.

I saw my clothes were badly torn. I wondered if the girl in trouble had, in fact, been me, so I ran, holding back a rising gorge, to the toilet, vomited and checked. Nothing about my privates seemed disturbed or different. There were no foreign substances. My underpants, though not fresh from the line, were intact and so, I knew, was my virginity.

As the grim anticipation that I'd been raped fell away, I relaxed, slumped toward a small low mirror (*all* mirrors are low for me) and saw with renewed horror my face. The muck on my hair was dried gore, and under my poor pug there were traces of a nose bleed. Both eyes were black. Forgotten tears had streaked lines into my stained cheeks. One of my ears had suffered damage. If I had no face for grief, I certainly had no face for debauchery. All I could do was ridicule that bopped and bruised visage.

"Too ugly even to be raped. Ho ho ho," I chortled sadly. "Maybe there's an advantage to that mug of yours after all."

But by the time I got back to Archibald's table, those guffaws had turned to sobs.

"What?" he said, pulling on the dirty fists that covered my eyes. "Hey, come on now, you laughin' or cryin', gal?"

I blubbered something, an indistinguishable sound.

"Yeah," he said.

Viewed through my tears in that purple outfit, he looked like an enormous grape advertising some new jam.

"Like me and Darlene a couple nights ago. We're fightin' and carryin' on. And she says, 'You're always laughin'. I'm sick to death of your damn jokes. I'm sick to death of YOU.' And I says, 'I ain't laughin', Darlene honey, I'm cryin.' And I was too. I sure was. Tears and all. Truth is," he said, (he even smelled like a grape, a slightly fermented grape ready for the wine vat), "Truth is, you might say, it was a LITTLE A BOTH!"

He pealed a laugh and slapped my back so hard that the shattered pieces which had been my shoulders relocated, sending a spasm of relief up my neck and out my throat in a combination burp and giggle.

I felt the stupor of those boilermakers as they rode up and down in my gullet making a fool of me. "Oh God," I burbled. I thought I was going to be sick again.

"No one's ever going to love me," I moaned. "They didn't even want to rape me."

I was maudlin drunk. I was sobbing so uncontrollably that Archibald thought someone had, in fact, raped me. The JFK girls gathered around to stare sympathetically at my misery. They knew instinctively it could only have been caused by men.

"WHA? THEM SONS A BITCHES!" Archibald roared.

His face went the color of his suit first (purple) and his Stetson next (white). "I told them sons a bitches at the Peace Crap they couldn't leave a gal out there by herself."

"I wasn't by myself," I sniveled. "Wally Martin was there." Oh what a great gush of tears came then.

"Let it come," the puce cowboy said softly. "Let it come, sweetheart, it's the oney way to git it all out."

Unfortunately, while I was getting it all out, he was pouring more in. His theory of fighting fire with fire was the talk of a pyromaniac.

I have no recollection of the ride from Makele to the capital, save the stops when I would puke and Archibald would throw tepid coffee into me from a bottomless thermos. I was no doubt reeking of whiskey, despite the after-shave lotion and spearmint gum that Archibald recommended, "to save that ol' Stout Margie from facing up to what she don't like to face up to about her kids." He dropped me into the lap of Margie Stout at the medical office, not two minutes before the close of work.

Margie deposited me directly into the Seventh-Day Adventist Hospital, where I was treated for concussion, abrasion, a broken rib and mild shock. Then, as if trying to mark my ignominy, the bums shaved my head.

6. Hi, I'm Cheryl Chaiken

It was right after lunch the next day when they wheeled in another patient. An American lady, the nurse said, a tourist. She had been attacked by wild animals and had just had plastic surgery. Her face was covered by bandages, a shock of short, thick gray hair bristled from the top of her head. One of her legs was in a cast.

"Wild animals?" I asked.

"Those awful baboons with the red chests," the nurse answered. She sighed, tucked the poor woman in and left me the lunch tray of the damned. Seventh-Day Adventists bring all their food in from their kitchens in Loma Linda, California. It's all made of soybeans.

Within a few minutes a woman arrived and dropped a flight bag and a raincoat over the foot of the fallen tourist.

"Hi, I'm Cheryl Chaiken," she said. "Jeee-sus what happened to you? They told me outside you were a Peace Corps volunteer. They beat you up out there or something? I don't know how you kids put up with it. You're all saints. Living saints of the twentieth century. What's your name?"

"Sarah," I said. It was a word in edgewise.

"Look at this, will you, Sarah," she sighed. She pointed to the woman in the next bed.

"Piece of luck though; there's an Australian plastic surgeon here. A first-rate guy. You would *not* believe it. I mean, I *talked* to this guy. I know. What makes a guy leave all that money behind in Sydney and come out to a place like this, work for nothing? Saints," she repeated.

Not more than five feet tall, she tromped with a short woman's efficiency and energy, checking I.V. bags, peering at bandages and muttering, "First-class. First-class."

"Listen, Sarah, will you do me a favor? In case she wakes up, tell her Mrs. Chaiken was here. Everything is arranged. She'll be back in Tenafly in her own apartment by noon on Monday, I promise. Tell her I'll be around later. You'll do that won't you?

"Piece of luck having an American right here in the room with her. You know, so she doesn't wake up and see a lot of foreigners." She drew a deep breath and said, "You probably even speak the language around here being in the Peace Corps and all that," and left.

The flight bag on the end of the woman's bed was bright turquoise. On the side printed in white letters were WOW and under that, discreetly, Worlds Out of this World, Chaiken Tours. A large tag on the handle said Mrs. Brenda Allen, 6700 Waterbury Blvd, Tenafly, New Jersey, Vanishing Species: World Wildlife No. 6—Colobus Monkey, Bleeding Heart

Baboon, Walia Ibex, Oryx, White Rhino, Bongo, Mountain Gorilla. On the woman's coat was a Save-the-Whales button and a little plastic pin saying Friends of the Bleeding Heart Baboon.

Before Mrs. Brenda Allen came to, Cheryl returned, peered in, whispered, "She still out of it?" and burst into the room.

"Yup," I answered.

She gasped. "Wow, hey, I forgot about you! Isn't someone going to bring you a wig or something?"

"They're trying to keep me in here, I guess," I said.

"Here look, try this."

She handed me a scarf picturing some ancient monument, the logo WOW in a decorative border. "Machu Picchu," she said, reaching to tie the thing behind my head.

The damn scarf wouldn't tie around my head so, giving up, she rested it on my ears. From certain angles I must have looked like an elephant nun.

"Anybody ever tell you you have a model's bone structure?" she asked me. "I mean your face," she said. "Have to flatten those ears."

"Who me?"

"Yeah," she said. She ogled me from below, framing my face with her hands. "From this angle you could pass for Leni Archimedes, cover of *Vogue* last month. Take off your glasses."

"Uh-uh," I said. "I never take off my glasses."

"You can't see without them, right? Man, if I could take off some glasses and go blind, I'd do it. What a headache I got. I mean, I have been *flat out* since this happened. What a piece of luck! Between this one and the fellow we've got on the coast with a heart attack. I've got to get the two of them the hell out of here and take care of the rest. We've got maybe fifty in this country right now. Don't ever let anybody con you into running tours, Sarah. It's nothing but a nightmare. Want some coffee?"

She pulled a thermos from a basket. Huffed and phewed it open and poured some into two plastic cups.

"Creamer?" she asked. "I mixed the sugar in the creamer," she said. "I find most people who want cream want sugar, and most people who don't want cream don't want sugar. If you only want sugar, sweetheart, you're out of luck, or vice versa."

"I drink it black," I said.

"See, I was right." She stirred her coffee, blew on it and put it down. A moan came from Brenda Allen. Then silence.

"I don't mind telling you in this business we get a lot of accidents. It's the nature of the kind of tours we run. I mean we're trying for something different. Out of this world, right? We get a lot of old folks. I don't have to tell you that, do I? Let's face it, they're the only ones with money to burn. Lots of them want provision for a funeral, just in case.

"We did one in Rangoon. A Buddhist thing. It was fabulous. The old man's kids were hassling us to bring the body back, but there it was in his will. If he died on tour, he wanted to be buried on tour. This guy was like eighty-two! Fabulous, right? I'm not even going to make fifty-two at this rate."

There was another moan from Brenda Allen.

"What happened to *her?*" I asked.

"Oh, she's O.K. She got a little too friendly with a baboon baby, wanted to cuddle it or something." Cheryl Chaiken rolled her eyes. "These people, you shouldn't give them passports. They got no brains. I mean, phew! doesn't everybody know about maternal instinct?"

"Friends of the Bleeding Heart Baboon?"

"Yeh," Cheryl Chaiken rolled her eyes again. "We do these things for World Wildlife. They promote the tours, we run them, they get a cut. Like I say, we have a *lot* of accidents. Last year we had this old guy stuck on a rhino's horn. This guy thought the rhino could tell he was one of the good guys. He wanted to kiss it maybe. They had to kill the rhino, so what do you have? Save the Rhino? I'm always telling Charlie, my husband, let's get out of World Wildlife, *please.*"

Brenda Allen came to with a loud scream. *"My face!"* She was sitting up in bed with a hand on the bandages. *"My eyes!"* she yowled.

"Open your eyes, Mrs. Allen. It's Cheryl Chaiken. You're O.K. You're fine. You're practically on the plane . . ."

"Waaaaaaaah," Brenda Allen cried. "I can't see!"

"Come on now, Mrs. Allen," Cheryl took the quivering hand gently and lowered it. "Come on, you're O.K. Just *o-pen* your eyes."

Mrs. Allen opened her eyes. "Where am I?" she asked.

"Practically on the plane," Cheryl repeated.

"Where am I?" she shrieked, thumping her plastered leg on the bed.

"At the Seventh-Day Adventist Hospital!" Cheryl yelled. "Your doctor's an Australian. There's an American in here with you, a Peace Corps volunteer. Come on, there's nothing to worry about."

Mrs. Allen moaned and sank back into her bed.

"Thank you, Cheryl," she said. "But what about the others?"

"The others have gone ahead to see the oryx."

"You mean I'm going to *miss* the oryx?"

She sobbed.

"You can come another time. Mrs. Allen, you are very lucky to be alive."

"I don't have money for another time. This is my once in a lifetime trip. I don't want to go back to New Jersey until I see the oryx."

Mrs. Allen rolled to her side, groaned and started sniveling.

"Mrs. Allen, Worlds Out of this World has gone through a lot of trouble to get you this passage. Believe me, you'll be better off in your own home until you recover."

Mrs. Allen said nothing.

"Mrs. Allen, I've kept your luggage in my hotel room. Day after tomorrow I will collect you and you go directly from here to the airport. There are a lot of stitches in your face. Your arm is broken and your leg is fractured. That was a very big baboon dragging you over some very rough ground."

"I hope no one shot a gun at that baboon on my account," she said.

"The baboons are all fine, Mrs. Allen. Our guides fired into the air."

"Well, thank heaven for that," Mrs. Allen said.

She nodded her head and slept again. When she woke it was late afternoon. A nurse came, removed Mrs. Allen's I.V. and brought in our supper trays, composed entirely of thinly disguised soybeans.

"What happened to you?" Mrs. Allen asked.

I told her, "I was attending a ceremony. A dance. It got a little out of hand."

"I see," she said. "I suppose you Peace Corps volunteers really *must* attend these ceremonies, mustn't you? In order to establish rapport?"

"Yes," I answered.

"But you are O.K.? You're not hurt badly?"

"Oh no," I said.

"Well thank heaven. There's always a risk if something is going to be worthwhile." She sighed.

I could see a pout develop even under the bandages.

"It isn't fair for them to make me go home." She pushed the fried soybean patty around on her plate. It was awash in a thin reddish sauce that had no taste.

"Are you teaching them English?" she asked.

"I guess I'm teaching everything," I said. "I'm the only teacher in a little village."

"How wonderful." She put some of the patty into her mouth but couldn't get it down.

"I can't get this down," she complained. Her spoon pitched under the soybeans vinaigrette but she couldn't get those down either.

"I see you've eaten this food," she said. "I suppose you Peace Corps volunteers have to be prepared to eat and drink many strange new foods." She looked at my empty plate with envy.

"Do you live in one of their houses? In one of those dirty places?" she asked.

"Well, they only *look* dirty because they're made of mud bricks. Like adobe."

"You live just like the people then, you really do." She was managing to eat a bite or two of soybeans in curry gravy.

"I couldn't have done it. Even when I was your age." She dabbed her mouth with her napkin.

"But you know what would have scared me? The people. Not any of this business about dirty places and terrible food. I would have been frightened of the people. They're just so different. I suppose it's not their fault."

Next morning I was feigning sleep, waiting for Margie Stout to come get me out. You get no stimulants like coffee or tea in a Seventh-Day Adventist Hospital, and I had no real desire to face a day that began with soy grits, soy muffins and grain beverage.

I was somewhere in the alpha zone between sleeping and waking when I heard a man's voice say, "I'm terribly sorry that our baboons have done this to you."

What? I thought this guy was talking to me, taking cheap shots at my friends in Jiru.

"Hey, pal, you just wait a minute . . . ," I blurted, springing to life with such a jolt that my two legs shot out like broken springs from under the sheets.

I was so embarrassed by my bony knees and hollow thighs that I temporarily forgot my mowed and battered noggin, which, remembering, I endeavored to cover by grabbing for a towel that hung near my bed on a peg, causing my hospital johnny to open to the world baring my scanty chest. Cheryl Chaiken rushed to me with her Macchu Picchu scarf, muttering hazy good mornings and introducing me as Sarah Easterday to Mr. Zerahun of the Ministry of the Interior.

When I got my glasses on, I found myself looking at a familiar face. "Oh God, it's you," I said.

It was that fledgling aristocrat who had carried my note from Adi-Duri to Margery Stout.

He turned his princely face my way and recognized me, bald and bleary as I was.

"You are hurt!" he announced.

"So you know each other? Mr. Z. is our wildlife contact here," Cheryl Chaiken said. "He's been kind enough to come and make sure Mrs. Allen is O.K." She nodded, smiling in the direction of Mrs. Allen.

"Yes, how kind," Mrs. Allen said. "You really didn't have to do that, Mr. Zeraham."

"We were all concerned as to your welfare," Zerahun said.

If he hadn't done me such a favor, his snotty tone would have rolled around in my stomach like a squirt of lemon in a glass of milk.

"You mustn't blame the baboons," Mrs. Allen told him.

"Certainly not," Zerahun answered. "Nevertheless, our ministry will have to take more precautions with tourists. I feel we were remiss. The man escorting you should never have allowed you to leave the vehicle."

He sounded embarrassed, though the source of his embarrassment was obscure.

Chaiken, on the other hand, was obviously embarrassed by Mrs. Allen. "Mrs. Allen never should have tried to pick up a baby baboon. It goes without saying."

"Yes, but the babies are *so* cute," Mrs. Allen whined.

Zerahun turned to me, "And your friend?" he asked. "I hope he is well. I delivered your note immediately when I returned."

He saw in my face my news was bad, turned away before I could speak.

"He died," I whispered.

A thin liquid line of shadow drew his magnificent profile against the white light of the window behind him. A pedigree, immaculate, refined by centuries of breeding in this hidden empire, high in Africa.

He didn't ask what happened. He said, "I have always believed that this Peace Corps of yours should not be here." He shrugged. "But you're everywhere, aren't you?"

"What's this?" Cheryl Chaiken interrupted.

"Someone died? A friend of yours? A car crash?" She put her hand on her forehead and leaned back, phewing.

"Don't think it hasn't dawned on me. If there's a crash out there, you just lie in the road. I mean, phew, even if someone does come round, there's no hospital out there. People drive like crazy around here. Kiss it goodbye," she said. She kissed it goodbye.

"He had a mysterious fever," I told her.

"Don't even tell me what it was," Chaiken said. "I don't want to hear it. Green monkey fever? Dengue? Black water? *Why* do we come here?"

She held her palms out, phewed, and dropped to a chair.

"I'm sorry," Zerahun said.

He faced me solemnly, that ducal brow high and wide, his hair compressed, tense in a tight hard cap around his head.

I was not entirely convinced that he was sorry.

Margie Stout came with a blond curly wig (all she had) and a bright green dress (too wide and too short) that made me look like a cross between Harpo Marx and a praying mantis. A nurse laughed and a doctor told me to stay around town and report any severe headaches that might crop up in the next few weeks. Margery was pressing me to leave Jiru for good.

"We can place you somewhere else," she said. "This food business is worse than we think. People are starting to call it a famine. The UN is looking into it. There are beggars all over the city. Peace Corps would like to have all of you where we can watch out if something happens . . . ," and on and on she went, but it was no use.

The only thing I wanted to do was go back to Jiru so I could finish the road.

Margery was not sure, she said, whether the director would *let* me go back to Jiru, but I hung my head with an awful pout, shoulders sagging, boohoo.

And what about what Wally wanted, I asked, sniveling and miserable, until she finally gave up.

"Oh, do as you like, but don't be surprised if we don't let you."

Of course, I knew they couldn't stop me.

7. I have been known to count my chickens before they hatch

The sky that day was too magnificent to think of famines and cities full of beggars. There were clouds dancing up there and those angry and hungry northern towns seemed far away. I left that hospital as fast as I could, landed on the street and felt the uplifting bounce of going out *in-cog-nito,* capped as I was in platinum curls, the outsize green dress swirling like a dancer's. I didn't care about the odd bandage here and there, the exposé of knobbed and scabby knees, the full view afforded of my craggy ankles, feet shod in dirty tennis shoes.

I strutted down the main drag brandishing imaginary medallions, decorations signifying battles won, felt I was stepping on the fallen armies of my own transgressions. Yes, Easterday, my girl, back to Jiru. No more brawling and mooning and boozing alone. There was work to be done. The road to nowhere must be followed to its end. And Ho! Ho! *Tum-dee-dum!* You, Shoulders, are the one to do it. *Tah-dah!* Like that, until I saw from a distance that someone, in fact, had recognized me, was breaking a circle of friends and coming toward me.

He entered the field of my vision, smiled, put out a hand and said, "I see you bought a wig!"

It was Zerahun, with the sun in his bright black eyes.

I was struck shy and blushed. Uttered foolish uh-huh and tee-hee sounds and said, "Yes, everything's borrowed," indicating the green dress.

Something odd passed down my spine as far as it could go and then tingled up the other side until it reached a pit in my stomach, but only after fluttering a bit in my nether regions. "I didn't think anyone would recognize me."

"Well," he laughed, "not too many girls are reaching such a height."

"Oh, yes, well . . . ," I said.

"But where are you going now. Not so soon to Jiru?" he asked.

"No, not yet. I'm on my way to the Princess Zikaye," I told him. That run down fleabag slum-view hotel where the Peace Corps volunteers always stayed.

I was about to walk away, but he reached for my arm and held my wrist. His fingers were rich on my skin, and arrogant, as if they knew they had achieved all that my freckles strived for in vain, to cover me in warm brown.

"Tomorrow is Sunday," he said. "There is a bus that goes to the city limits and from there it is only a short walk to the waterfalls. Have you visited there?" He kept my arm in his hand.

Was this an invitation? A *date?* I wondered if he could feel that thin limb under his touch glowing like a neon light at the end of a dark street.

I could hardly breathe, and though I had once authored, produced, directed and secretly starred in a little one-man-one-act called "The Flirt" (an ironic mime), I could not find a way to respond to this man. I remembered the wig which laughed at my comic face, and the green dress which made a joke of my knee-caps, and I simply nodded in agreement. Without even a smile.

"Then I will come to meet you at the Princess Zikaye at eleven."

He loosened his grip, but my wrist refused to fall away, hovered shamelessly under his touch, its reddish hairs at attention, its freckles embedded in a deep blush.

I nodded again. Was my mouth slung open, my eyes wide with wonder? I felt cool air on my tongue. My retinae were doing sit-ups.

Later in the pocked and pitted mirror of the ladies' bath at the Zikaye, I looked it over—my body—in hope that those hormones which had surged at Zerahun's touch had caused some miraculous change, some late blooming. But no. Things were worse than ever.

Like most full-length mirrors, hung at some average height, this one lopped off my face, spared me my head (thank God) with its fringe of stubbled scalp. There was only a body which moved like a marionette, and like a marionette's body, it was meant to be clothed. If I threw my weight to one hip, the other flared outward and I could see down one side a soft womanly contour, waist and hip swell. But could I go around posed thus, slung to one side like a catatonic, for the sake of those curves? And if I pressed my arms against my sides and leaned in on my chest, my breasts rolled together, gathering flesh from my rib cage and swelling slightly like those white orbs the poets sing about. Oh, bah, could I go around crimped toward my center in a vise of arms for the sake of a cleavage?

Whoever took me would have to take me as I am, or not (sigh) at all. But if it was going to be this Zerahun (I have been known to count my chickens before they hatch), I was game. I had heard a lot of Peace Corps Macho, in the spirit of run-the-competition-down, about how these guys were after white ass. Any white ass at all. Which sounded like a perfect description of my ass.

But when I saw Zerahun in the lobby of the Zikaye next day, I grew fainthearted. Those eyes notwithstanding, I didn't think I liked him much. He was part of the reason things were so bad in his country. He held a small cup of espresso coffee to his lips, the long nail on his baby finger proclaiming that he did no manual labor. There was a heavy gold ring on it. He wore a black turtleneck jersey and an emerald green pullover. The colors were perfect for his Byzantine face. A barefoot street boy in rags squatted in front of him polishing his shoes. When the boy finished, Zerahun leaned forward to check the job, patted the boy's head, then handed him a coin. As he sat back upright his face passed a shaft of light and his beauty was astonishing, but it looked sinful somehow, like a price, not a gift, and for a split second, I was glad of my awkward shape and homely features.

Except for a greeting, we walked in silence and waited in silence for the bus. When it came it was almost empty, like the streets abandoned for the churches, the morning-long services echoing chants along the high ridges from holy loudspeakers, over the deep crowds gathering in the churchyards, and over the beggars, leprous and blind, that lined the way.

"That poor Mrs. Allen," Zerahun said by way of small talk.

He offered me a cigarette. I turned it down.

"But aren't you a friend of the bleeding heart baboons?" I asked him.

He laughed. "You know, I don't know anything about those

baboons. I was not trained in wildlife. In my country if you are trained in one thing, they make sure to give you a job in something else."

"You were trained in—?"

"Political Science," he said. He grinned sarcastically, but not at me, straight ahead as though he were looking at the ghost of someone who had tricked him.

"At Cornell University in New York. When my father learned of my studies, he brought me immediately home. I was supposed to be learning about agronomy. My father has farmlands which are being ruined by his tenants. Now my brother has gone to learn agronomy. At Purdue University. In Illinois." He inhaled deeply, stared for awhile out the window at the houses.

The population thinned as we passed out of the city.

"Tell me," he said, "about what you do in Jiru. You know, we go to your country and you come to ours, and we still know nothing about each other. I find it strange that you would go out there."

"This is going to sound funny," I told him. "But once I was caught in a terrible flood. In Kansas. My mother and I were rescued. So I figure I owe something."

"You came out here to rescue us?" He chuckled.

I felt the old lump in my throat: he was laughing at me, sending my purpose down the drain. I knew if I tried to talk, I'd only gurgle and whinny like a sick horse. So I shrugged my shoulders. They felt bigger than ever and the shrug clattered at my collar bone and shivered to my elbows far away.

"And your friend? Did he come out here to rescue us?"

"I dunno," I muttered. There was something bitter in my mouth now, dissolving the lump. "Maybe he just came out here to look at the southern skies. *He* was *trained* in astronomy."

"You're angry?" he asked.

He put a single finger on my shoulder, which twitched in Morse code and sent an exciting message to my heart.

"You're naive," he said.

I stared at his turtleneck jersey, black against the brown of his neck, a skin that bloomed with gold.

"So what?" I asked. This time I looked straight into his eyes.

"None of you should be here," he said. "It's ridiculous."

"But you have nothing to say about it," I told him.

After a while the bus stopped. The driver stood up, stretched and climbed down. We could see him wander off, a man looking for a place to take a leak. It was the end of the line.

I was tempted to stay on and ride back to town, but I followed Zerahun out, jumped to the earth, breathed deeply of an air heavy with the smell of eucalyptus, like a breath of cough drops, adjusted my silly locks and asked "Which way?"

He pointed down the road and walked ahead of me. Shallow ditches fell away on both sides and in them I could see women bent like beasts, combing the ground for trash, each with a load of pitiful sticks and scraps of paper tied to her back. Oh God! it made me sad to see them. But what could I do?

Beyond those bent women, I saw houses locked in walled compounds, hidden behind iron gates among big trees and lush gardens.

Zerahun was talking to a group of people who stood in front of the first gate.

As I approached, he walked to the middle of the road, passing in a wide arc around the people who now turned to stare at me.

It was a poor family—a woman, a man and three children. Their clothes were dirty, the children were naked. They watched as I walked by them, as I swung out into the street after

Zerahun, greeting them tentatively as I passed. The woman smiled and bowed to return my greeting.

"What are those people doing?" I asked.

He grinned, again maliciously, again at some ghost that hovered near him, a weak conscience that calls you guilty, but won't let you make amends.

"They're begging," he said. "What do you think?"

"They don't seem like beggars," I said.

They didn't. They weren't petulant, demanding. They merely looked stunned.

"You're right," he said. "They've never done it before."

"Will they beg at that house, at the door?" I asked.

"Yes, if they can get in."

"Who lives there?"

"Even they asked me this. I told them the Minister of Culture and Social Work lives there. And he deserves them, too." He laughed. "It's an old custom. He has to give them money and food, or they will strip in his driveway. To strip naked, this is humiliating. To do this shows they are finished."

"Will he give them something?"

"He will," Zerahun said. "If they should die naked in his driveway, everyone would know he refused to give. That would never do. He'll give them enough to get them to the next house. Then when it starts raining, they'll go home. It's an old story."

"You don't like this, do you?" I could see his distaste that this was happening and that I was seeing it.

But he shook his head and then said, almost lightly, "It will be just like China. They army will come into power. It's a matter of history. They'll kill the royals, the landlords, they'll kill the ministers, they'll kill the intellectuals. They'll kill my family. They'll kill me."

I didn't want anyone getting killed: it pained me to hear it put that way. Was history all about one side killing the other? And it seemed Nature, gone wild, did nothing but aggravate this sad reality. I had read what the tidal waves and typhoons had done to the Bay of Bengal—a million dead, in the aftermath of flood and bloody civil war. And here, this famine which no longer was contained. It was waiting in the driveways of the rich.

"If it came to that," Zerahun said, and he looked so sad, as though it was not his fault, "would you be inclined to rescue me?"

I noticed that the rolled edge of his black turtleneck was worn, that the elbows of his emerald green sweater hadn't long to live.

"Well, yes." I glowed, something girls who are six-foot-two should never do, especially while wearing the blonde wigs of nurses.

"Don't be surprised if I call on you." But he was joking.

The waterfall was, among other things, a lover's lane. Half-hidden in the trees and bushes, couples were doing what couples do, dim shades, movement and dream, like my own expectations along those lines. It embarrassed me to my very root. I felt the follicles of my outraged hair tingle under that foolish wig.

"The Italians used to come here for picnics," Zerahun said.

He brushed leaves from an old stone bench, chased away a few ragged kids who had gathered to gawk at us and motioned me to sit down.

"It's nice," I said.

I gulped at the words because there again in my throat, strangely, was a lump. Oh goodness, why? It must have had something to do with that sad cascade of water, dark in the blue-red shade, its lush jungle plants breathing, its violet mists, and the pool at its base in a platinum circle of light.

Along the edge of the river that crawled slowly from that bright pool, however, were the inevitable piles of shit because the waterfall was also a public toilet. Yes—yes, we all know that love and excrement share the same region of the body, so why not share the waterfall? But still . . . I wished, as all fallen angels wish, that we could do just a little better.

Out of nowhere Zerahun said "You know, you Americans have such sentimentality about animals. Friends of the Bleeding Heart Baboon! Well, it's alright, I suppose." He gazed ahead—that presence; it was always with him. "But have you ever seen our great ground hornbills?"

I had. There were people in Jiru and Bari-Cotu who kept ground hornbills around, something like outpatient pets. Forget canaries and parakeets, these huge buggers barked like dogs and chased sticks. Regular clowns. Tesfa had a couple which must have been four feet tall, like midget clerics with Jimmy Durante noses. They rarely flew, but when they did, we could hear the whoosh of their great wings stirring the wind through the valley beyond.

Everyone claimed that hornbills mated for life. Their paternal instinct is strong, none of this wham-bam-thank-you-ma'am that normally characterizes reproduction. The male seals up his lady and their eggs in a little cave or hollow tree and faithfully feeds her through a tiny opening just big enough for her bill. When every egg has hatched, they break the seal. The mother tumbles out, fat and flightless from inactivity.

Zerahun said, "We are finding the females sealed up and dead. The males cannot range far enough to find food for them. They do not understand what is happening to them, they can only go on as they have always done. It is like my country—sealed and dead."

Sadly, the day looked as though it were going to be one for philosophy, not love. The brooding Coptic eyes of this Zerahun did not inspire the frivolous in me, and my goggled peepers no doubt did not inspire the lover in him. He mused, sat like Rodin's *The Thinker,* with his chin on his fist.

We both mused, growing tired and bored, when through the undergrowth, like a wagon train breaking into Old Missouri, came first the nasal sounds of New Jersey and then the whole gang of them wearing their turquoise caps and matching windbreakers all marked WOW.

Cheryl Chaiken was bringing up the rear in a loud *entre nous:* "The Italians were lousy colonialists. They never *did* anything with the place. All this potential and what do you get? A bunch of roads and picnic spots. There's a massacre story about this one," she said.

"You wanna hear a massacre story? Down there, you can see the remains of a vineyard—hopeless, anyone will tell you you can't make wine here. Well after the war, when it was *Get the Italians* time, zap zap zap, three families. It's not over. I mean *these* people are bloodthirsty. Believe me, you only have to look at the way they treat animals."

She paused, changed her tone and yelled "Find a spot for your picnics everyone. You've got fifteen minutes."

As she settled, opening her satchel and pulling out a white cardboard lunch box, signed like a work of art: Hilton, she spotted first Zerahun and then me.

"Jeee-sus," she said.

She laughed. "Hey, listen, excuse me, but that wig is *not you,* honey."

I patted my coif in a mock primp. Zerahun said hello and other pleasantries.

She answered, "Phew! I nearly *killed* myself coming up that hill. Say, why don't you guys, you know, fix up this place. Develop it. Tables. A bar. Beer. Soft drinks. Maybe some quick food like shish kebabs—I'm not talking McDonald's or anything. Run tour buses through here. You could make a fortune."

She opened her box, extracted a hard-boiled egg, grimaced, and began looking for something else which she didn't find.

"Did Mrs. Allen leave?" I asked.

"Jeee-sus, don't remind me. Yeh-yeh, she left, but I've still got to get this group into Rwanda to see a mountain gorilla. I mean this whole show is Charlie's idea. See them before they're extinct! Chaiken's last chance tours. Charlie's got an idea a minute . . ."

She phewed and piffed and shook her head, offering around her lunch box which smelled of hard-boiled eggs.

"*Then* I get to do it all over again with the Audubon Society. WOW's Big Bird Walk. And where's Charlie? Doing the porny temples in India. I've had it."

She paused, made a face and said, "You ever see pictures of those temples? It's enough to make you convert."

She winked and stood and was on her way, a mother hen, fluffing her charges like overgrown chicks, and they followed her clucking and peeping.

"Bye now!" she shouted back at us. And they were gone.

Zerahun said something derogatory about Americans which I ignored, but as we left, he took my hand, leading me down the hill of Chaiken's complaint, and with his thumb, stroked mine. I felt that soft stroking everywhere. No one had ever held my hand that way before.

On the way back we found the beggar family sitting under a shade tree near the Minister of Culture's gate. In front of them, on a greasy piece of newspaper, was the remains of a meal, some gnawed bones and scraps of flatbread. There were two tin can cups, half full of tea. They smiled as we drew near, the woman bowing from her waist, her head bobbing in respect and suspicion.

Zerahun asked them when they thought they might be able to go home. The man told him he wasn't going to go home. The Minister of Culture and Social Work had given him some money and an idea. He was going to buy some balloons, some string and some sticks and then, using his own air (which was free), blow up the balloons, tie them to the sticks and sell them for twice as much to parents on Sunday afternoons when they came with their children to see the emperor's lions. From his profits, he would buy more balloons and string and sticks and a bit of food, blow those up with more free air and sell them and so on until he was a rich man.

Zerahun said he thought it was a good idea and gave the man some more money. Since I didn't want to be left out of this deal, I dug into my pocket and invested as well.

"Balloons?" I asked Zerahun. "Did I hear that right? Balloons?"

8. Some air force colonels had moved into the palace

I saw Zerahun several times after that, but, sad to say, I returned to Jiru *the same.* Except that my hair had reached a quarter of an inch so I looked like Ichabod Crane joins the marines. Each time I had seen Zerahun, he was more and more nervous about what he called "his fate," something blurred and violent, ending with his death at the hands of a furious mob waving vicious red banners of revolution.

"Like China," he insisted.

He seemed at peace with the logic and inevitability of it. It was the only thing that could happen to his country if it didn't collapse, though he kept hinting that it had already collapsed. He was only troubled by the interim, and when he talked to me about rescue, it wasn't that he wanted to be saved from death, but from the hell of giving up his life before it was finished.

Oh what luck, Easterday! *This* was the character that finally appeared as your potential first love? *This* was the first man to hold your hand, to explore the electric chasm of your palm, to let you know that, yes-yes, it's true, fingertips *are* erogenous zones? *This man.* He was so sublimely unhappy and penetratingly depressed, I figured even Helen of Troy posed naked on his doorstep could not have succeeded. And Lord knows, I had none of Helen's skills.

And what about *my* fate? I felt doomed to wear a large red V on my chest like some upside-down Hester Prynne.

I was in no mood to travel back to Jiru. Even the Day-Glo pink interiors of the JFK didn't help. I half hoped to run into Archibald and his bottle, but no one save the girls were around. They were all horrified at the sight of my ravaged head, on which I was wearing nothing but a friendly old Franklin D. Roosevelt sort of white cotton hat.

Samayanesh rushed away and returned with a scarf to try to fix things up, make me look better, she said. She unfurled the piece of silken cloth. On it was a picture of Neil Armstrong in his spacesuit, walking on the moon. The earth hung behind him with a small hole eaten into it by one of the rats that live in the closets of the JFK. One small step for man: one giant step for mankind fluttered in front of my face like an advertisement.

Samayanesh knew all about it: "*That* is an American man," she said. "And *that* is the moon." She had no idea how he got up there or how he got back, and when I told her, she didn't seem very interested.

Oh how I missed Wally on that trip. I moped through Adi-Duri. I sulked into Bari-Cotu. I could hardly bear to put one foot in front of the other. Only the sight of our absurd road cheered me. It laughed at the world, at the famine, at the people in the cities in their neckties and big cars.

The folks in Jiru saw me coming. I was walking down the middle of their road, after all, like Agamemnon back from the Trojan Wars. Samayanesh's scarf hung under my FDR hat like an Arab's whatnot to keep the sun off my neck. First the small kids came skipping and yelping, shouting that I was back, and then it seemed like everyone was out in welcome and surprise. Both my hands were held tightly, by Alganesh on one side, and by Marta, her sister, on the other. Alganesh's baby rode on her back, hale as the day. It was one of those rare moments that spreads out, touches the tips of the horizon where rainbows end and leaps back to you. It was one of those rare moments, if you're ready for it, when you can believe nothing else matters, and I thought in the joy, pause, reach and lift of it, that *this* was love, and I was not so left out after all.

From my veranda the view promised renewed health. I saw, in a daydream, the blue-violet mesas bloom like wild gardens after the rains, the yellow shimmer of the highland September flowers. I even thought I saw the flicker of lightning break the sky, but it was only the sun's light, splintered by the parched air. Although a storm was brewing, there was no rain on the way.

It looked as though we had less than two months of work left on the road when Zerahun showed up in Jiru. He came dressed in old clothes, a torn jacket, and broken shoes, attempting, he said, to look like a student. He had hitched a ride in the back of a truck full of Food for Work. He told me he had quit the Ministry of the Interior, and had gotten into some political trouble. He was looking for a place to stay until a message came and then he would go north, possibly into the Sudan, possibly into exile.

That night we drank a lot of wine that he brought with him from the capital, wine the Italians still made in vineyards around the city. I swam first on its sweet bouquet and then I swam with the flow of it. Chaiken was wrong: the Italians were right. They could grow grapes and make wine in Africa.

It was past midnight when I staggered into my room to find some bedding for my guest. I brought it to him. He was all but undressed. His back was toward me, lean, rich with muscle, tapered to a hard tight waist. He wore white jockey shorts. His long back curved under the waistband, below it the round elastic curve of his flanks and then his legs, straight, so black in the dark shadows they were invisible. He seemed to float as he turned to face me and without embarrassment reached for the sickly gray pillow that dangled from my fists.

As though he noticed the way I was looking at him and felt obliged to say something, he said, "I had a lot of white girl friends at Cornell."

I was jealous. Odds were a million to one that they were all better looking than me.

"You all like to pretend you're so free, but you're really not.

You're not even honest—just curious about black boys, aren't you?"

He held the pillow against his chest, his arms around it, and I knew some girl back there had given him the business. It looked like she had siphoned off the profits and left me with the liquidation sale.

"I'm just curious in general," I said, or rather, I slurred.

He caught my drift, answered, "Well, you can forget about me. I'm useless," dropped the pillow and held his arms up like a hostage.

I didn't dare look. I thought of the famous artist, Ibrahim from Makele, whose balls had been removed and hung to dry in the sun by the wild tribes along the Omo River. Then I thought of the centuries of inbreeding that this aristocracy had lived through, the mad lascivious, and the mad ruined. But when I finally did look at him, he was all there. All there but not willing, I could tell at a glance.

I felt so washed up standing there thinking about him the way I did, but I wanted him. I wanted him so bad, as the saying goes, I could taste it. It was not to be.

A few days later word reached Jiru that there had been a coup. Tesfa came back from Adi-Duri with the news that some air force colonels had moved into the palace. They were arresting the evil people who had caused the suffering in the land all these years, Tesfa said. He was wrapped in his white homespun sheet like a biblical shepherd, and he stood with one leg up on a boulder as the crowd gathered to hear him.

It was unbelievable news, as strange to them as the story of the American man who had walked on the moon. I looked up toward my house and saw Zerahun standing there on a rise just where the road work had ended the previous day, and I knew, of course, that he was in on it somehow.

"What do you know about this?" I asked him.

"I was part of it," he said. "But they are treacherous." He seemed resigned, yet still fugitive. "Soon they will have to start the killing, and I will have to get out of this country."

"Egypt?" I said.

"France," he said morosely. He crossed his arms on his chest and hung his head. "I'm a member of the royal family."

"A prince?" I asked.

"No, not a prince: well, I suppose, in ways you could call my father a king. But it's nothing, an anachronism. I was willing to forget it but they weren't."

"How are you going to get out of here?" I asked.

"Well, I'll have to walk. Either north, as I have said, or down to the sea."

I slumped with the idea, felt the weight of my football player's shoulders as they accepted gravity and drooped in despair. "No," I said. "Why don't you stay here? No one is going to find you here."

Naturally I was wrong. The people in Jiru were marked by the recent events. They no longer had a king: it changed everything. Even though the king had done absolutely nothing for them, it seemed that God had fallen, that they were unprotected and in great danger.

But to Tesfa, who was spending lots of time in Adi-Duri, it seemed about time. He thought a new era had dawned, one he had been secretly dreaming of since a Peace Corps volunteer, five or six years ago, had told him about a place where each man had a vote. Tesfa was like a Jehovah's Witness, reborn, and the strange tongues that came from his mouth as he rolled in ecstasy had phrases in them like "root out all subversive elements."

Now, although Tesfa didn't know who Zerahun was, he knew a subversive when he saw one—a stranger with something to hide. And the truth of Zerahun's origins were carved unmistakably on his face. And so, in Adi-Duri, at a meeting of workers and peasants, Tesfa told about the aristocrat in the woodpile.

Things were happening fast. Peace Corps started sending me frantic messages that I was to return to the capital to wait until the situation returned to normal. The situation seemed perfectly normal to me, so I simply tore up their messages. Then Alganesh came and told us what Tesfa had done: the unthinkable. He had ratted on a guest.

Alganesh, though as demure and feminine as she was bred to be, was wise: Tesfa, like any spiteful revolutionary fisherman, was not going to let Zerahun be the big one that got away. If Zerahun tried to travel, she said, Tesfa would follow. *But* if Zerahun *hid* for a few days, Tesfa would *also* follow. *I.e.,* she wanted to send Tesfa on a wild-goose chase.

"Come with me," she said.

She was nimble in the dark, a tomboy's skill hidden under her yards and yards of skirt. As a child she must have wandered in these deep ravines that scarred the Jiru hills. Now, she bounded along the back hip of a long ridge that stretched to the east and the sea, as surefooted as her hidden goat.

I stumbled after her, all arms and legs and kneecaps, fell more than once and heard Zerahun whispering frantically behind me, "Do you trust her?"

She was already far below us, a white spot, like a puff of cotton or a dandelion pod caught by the wind and carried, whirling, downward. Her hurry pulled us along, made us trust.

"I can't stay long," she said. "My baby will cry and they will come to find me." She hopped along the bottom of the ravine to a small cave, a dark hole just big enough for a man if he sat or crouched. Matted dried grass was on the floor.

"There," she said.

"There?" I said. "There?"

She had meant well.

Zerahun peered in and from the dark pulled out a thick white piece of eggshell. "It's a ground hornbill's nest!" he said.

He looked startled, as though some premonition had come true, stooped, picked up a shard of clay, the hornbill's seal.

Alganesh handed him a bag of roasted wheat kernels.

Next morning I made it known—casually—that Zerahun had gone. I also made it known—casually—that although I wasn't sure, because he had simply disappeared in the night, I had heard him talking about going to fight with rebels in the north. Tesfa was as cool as I was, but Tesfa disappeared the next night.

I went immediately to Adi-Duri. It was market day and there were rumors of carrots, tomatoes and eggs. My idea was to call Archibald on the phone there and get him to send his helicopter or one of his cars to save Zerahun. Why I thought the phone would work and Archibald would agree, I'll never know. Rescuers, I was learning, are not always rational. If they were, they would go out of business.

Adi-Duri was strangely quiet. The story was that shortly after the coup, a revolutionary mob, elated with the confidence that everything was going to get better, that there really was enough to go around, raided all the stores, confiscated all the goats and sheep and distributed everything to the beggars. That must have been a wild night. A week later everyone was *still* hung over. A stupor hung in the air as though everyone was waiting for the new government to come in with the Alka Seltzer.

The little old man who kept the Adi-Duri phone alive was nowhere to be seen. The post office clerk, a young idealist, told me that I could go ahead and use the phone free of charge. "Everything," he said, "belongs to the *people* now, so there can be no charges."

The free phone, however, was comatose. A faint hum came from its wires, then a gasp, then a sputter, then a rattle, then nothing and then, again a hum. I shook it, shouted into it, pounded it, cursed it, and finally threw coins at it like a shopper driven mad with bargaining.

"Oh no!" An unexpected voice cracked behind me and I had the quick happy realization that rescuers, irrational or not, are often very lucky.

"You're not telling me the thing's out of order."

It was a voice as familiar, as American, as the Brooklyn Bridge.

"So this is where you live?"

"Good God!" I said. "Do you know there's been a coup?"

"In this business, we can't let that stop us. We had a group once stranded in the Hilton in one of those banana republics for a week. They *loved* it. Guns going all night. They didn't even complain when the food and water ran out."

"Listen," I said, getting right to the point. "Where are you going?"

"North," she said. "Right the hell out of here. We have a one-way permission slip. You want a lift?" She rolled her eyes and phewed. "When I get back to the city, I am going on sabbatical. Charlie says he wants to *relax* in the Bahamas. The Bahamas? I just want to breathe a little smog for awhile. Eat hamburgers. Am I nuts?"

"Please," I said. "It isn't me. It's Zerahun, Mr. Zerahun, your wildlife contact. He has to get out of here. It's life or death."

"Aw-right, aw-right," she said, sighing, nosing around in her great satchel in search of cigarettes. "I suppose it *had* to happen." She lit up. "Where is he?"

"Hiding," I told her.

"At your place? He's your boyfriend or something? Well, drag him out. We're only stopping for a twenty minute lunch. What a hole this is! Listen, sugar," she took my hand, "I mean it, you are a saint. There's no two ways."

"Actually, we have to go get him." I didn't want to go into details. I only wanted one of her cars and the driver.

She looked suspicious, sucked on her cigarette, but I could tell she was pudding and couldn't say no to anything.

"Let me have a car," I said.

We stepped onto the porch of the post office. Two turquoise VW buses were parked outside. WOW they said in foot high white letters. Inside them, spectral, glazed with astonishment behind the rolled up windows, were six white faces that wanted to go home.

I motioned in a noncommittal way. "Just over that track to a place called Bari-Cotu. No problem in dry weather. And then from there, there's a *brand new road* to Jiru. I can have him in the car fifteen minutes after we get there."

"Honey," she said blowing smoke in my face, "are you *serious?*"

"He's a prince," I said.

"Yeh, sugar, I bet he's a *prince* awright," she chuckled. "You like him."

"I love him," I said.

I said it softly, not like a lover because I wasn't one, but like a yearning woman and a friend. And she heard it! Oh, how pathetic I must have looked, that brush of hair, all my cowlicks standing at attention askew like a drunken battalion. But what a note that old word sounds. Love. She was toppled by it.

"O.K.," she answered. She was having second thoughts but suddenly she brightened. "You know, they're gonna love it! What a story! What a romance! Taking a black prince out to his exile. It's fabulous! Charlie will die. He'll keel over and die."

I bent down almost two full feet and hugged the shit out of Cheryl Chaiken.

When we passed Bari-Cotu and hit the smooth of the Jiru Road, the turquoise VW bus seemed to fly. They would all see it from the town, I thought, the first real traffic, bright as a semiprecious stone. If we hadn't been hurtling along, I would have got out and poured a libation to the gods that made that road possible: I would have bent down and kissed its dusty flanks. The driver, however, was pissed off.

"That madame," he said, meaning Chaiken, "will be very angry because we are so late."

I pushed through the pile of kids that fell on us as the bus stopped, and ran down the ravine. Zerahun was out, all forlorn, sitting on a stone, about to give up.

"I've got a car!" I shouted. "Going north."

"Oh?" he said. He continued to sit there like the lump in my throat incarnate. "Maybe I ought to stay here and meet my destiny," he said. "Men who try to escape their fates inevitably fail."

"Oh for God's sake!" I bellowed. *"Don't be such an ass!"*

I was fed up: his miserable destiny. I grabbed both his arms and pulled.

He rose but resisted, tears streaming from his wonderful black eyes. At first I felt the force of his resistance, but then my adrenalin overcame it and he fell, collapsed wailing, right on top of me. My arms were around him, and I was all mixed up between my desire to get him off me and into that turquoise chariot, and my instinct to keep him there and be his mate (an instinct which, even in such a suggestive position, he showed no signs of sharing.)

I held him, oh I held him, and stroked his head and, boohoo-hoo, we were both going to pieces, especially me because his elbow was pressing my bladder and I was sure I was about to wet my pants. What conflicts I was going through! A mess of tangled limbs, tangled emotions and tangled urges. I wanted to pee and to love, to fight and to play, to laugh and to cry, and damn, I think it all could have been accomplished, but we were pressed for time. I developed a sudden horrendous case of hiccups.

I hicked and jerked with Zerahun to the waiting car. I jammed him through the door and shook his hand. Hics and hoops punctuated my final words like the ticking of a clock. I didn't have time to hold my breath and count to fifty. It was all I could do through my tears and slurps and gulps to extract a promise that he would send me a letter as soon as he got to safety. I saw tears in his eyes and believed he did care for me and believed that we would meet again.

As the WOW bus sped away, I boohooed and hiccupped, a regular one-man band of sniffs and spasms that shook me from head to toe. I hupped in such agony that I felt like some foiled Greek heroine, victim of cosmic irony, sending my love down the very road (*the very road*) that I had built. A road built for rescue, but not, oh ye gods, not for *that* rescue. Carried away by an Hellenic impulse, I raised my arms and my voice hicked "Why me?" to the sparkling heavens.

There was no answer, but, at least, when I put my arms down, the hiccups were gone.

9. A memory leapt like the hairs on my forearms

I was hanging on in Jiru, missing Zerahun, missing Wally, but sticking to my guns when, as Jack Archibald put it, the shit hit the fan. The new regime, like all new regimes, wanted to get rid of all the vestiges of the old regime. That included the Americans, all of them, even the Peace Corps. We were given a deadline by which to get out or go to jail. But the post office in Adi-Duri, where everything was free of charge, had gone out of business, so the letter telling me to get my ass back to the big city or else never arrived. I was busy watching the last hundred feet of the Jiru Road with trepidation, thinking about what we could do next to keep the flow of Food for Work coming. Like: build a clinic. Did it matter that there were no doctors? Would the team of Neuter, Clapp and Lewis notice? I could visualize that clinic, shining white, a landmark between Bari-Cotu and Jiru along the new road. Perhaps, once it was built, a doctor would show up.

It was a time for lazy daydreams like that. We had lost all hope of ever seeing rain again; roofs went unrepaired, gaping to the empty sky. We learned how to bathe using a cup of water, like Bedouins in the Sahara. There was no way to carry out the simple time-consuming routines that require water, no way to do the laundry. The drops we coaxed from our reluctant wells were parceled out. As they dwindled, so our lives slowed down, nearly stopped.

And all the while the horizon was thickening in such a subtle, one might almost say, sneaky and malevolent way, that it went unnoticed. Who knows how long? No clouds were released to float around like good omens, like tidings of great joy.

One day as I sat on my veranda, giving an English lesson based on the great Dr. Seuss classic *Bartholomew Cubbins and the Five Hundred Hats,* I saw, on the smooth tops of those distant mesas, a heavy blue-gray slash as though a mad artist had dragged his brush across the sky. A memory leapt like the hairs on my forearms from that timeless self that remains infant, child, adult—Kansas, the yellow prairie and the far horizon where the big floods come from.

I stopped midsentence, just as the executioner was in hot pursuit of Bartholomew's head, which was producing nonstop, wilder and more glorious hats. Kids thumped on the book the way kids do when their reader so much as pauses to draw a breath. They thumped and I stared westward until they all looked up, following my eyes to the mesas, and saw. That night a damp cold wind blew from the west, and in the morning, the tablelands were hidden for the first time since I had come to Jiru.

I never felt more than the first few drops of the rain which finally came to Jiru and the valleys around in ruinous black sheets. I was on my way, with Alganesh and her sister Marta, to Adi-Duri where we had heard there was a new supply of sugar and some dried meat. It was cold and weird that day. We could see the rain, wide vertical pillars of falling water along the western horizon. The pillars seemed to be holding up the sky which was a clear icy blue, a platform for the burning highland sun. We didn't know whether to be jubilant or afraid. We didn't know whether to hope for the storm's arrival or pray for its retreat. We didn't know whether to celebrate or curse, laugh or cry. Alganesh, sensing trouble, left her baby home, but Marta was gay. Though her dress was tattered and dirty, she looked like a butterfly, her white skirt with its bright embroidered border remembered the day it was new and put on a show for us.

We were just about at the bottom of the Jiru hill when we saw Archibald's whirlybird. It jumped into the air over the houses of Bari-Cotu, flew along the road toward us. We waved our arms at it and it lowered. Archibald hung out one side like the last raspberry of summer in a vermillion cowboy suit, motioning frantically that we should go back to Jiru right away. The copter righted itself, rose and knacka-knacka-knacka-knacked up to wait for us in its parking place near the school.

"What in hell's the matter with you, gal?" Archibald roared. (I was coming up the hill as he hollered.) "You as goddamn stupid as you look?" he said. "Wha, I said to that ol' Stout Margie, jest how long are you gonna wait on that dumb gal? She's ain't oney as tawl as my wife, I said, she's as damn pigheaded. Now pack your bag and git in this machine."

"Huh?" I said.

Before I could think, I had to catch my breath and adjust my glasses which had lost the bridge of my nose and were causing me to see double, two bright Jack Archibalds like cherries on a banana split. I figured he had heard a bad weather report and was coming to rescue me from the approaching flood.

"Listen, don't worry about me," I said.

I was close to him, looking at the ground and I whispered,

"You can't expect me to go and leave everyone else behind. How would that look?"

"I purely CAN expect it. I order it."

"Hey, wait a minute. You can't order me around." I turned to walk away.

"What IS the matter with you GAL? You lost your sense? Don't you think them commies mean business?"

Oh what a piteous whine that man had. It must have been the tone he used when he pleaded with Darlene. Only I wasn't deaf to it. It was too lonely, scared, and pathetic to ignore.

I went back to him. "A little rain isn't going to bother me," I told him.

"I ain't talkin' about RAIN," he said in that same lost tone, a kid who's done it all wrong and wants to make it up. "Naw, it ain't RAIN I'm talkin' about. I'm talkin' about the commies down there in the capital. Wha, they're gonna kick all us Americans outa here!" He seemed surprised.

"Even ME!" he added as though he thought, since he had bought drinks for everyone, they should love him and want him to stay.

"An' I had friends too," he told me, "in some very high places. Don't you forgit it 'cause I ain't gonna forgit it. This ol' Jack don't take things light." He was revving, voice loud again, belly proud. He patted it.

"Ain't nothin' LIGHT about me 'cept when I'm LIT!" He guffawed, slapped my back and grabbed my arm.

"You come on, now," he said.

"We're being expelled?" I asked. "Banished? Deported?"

"That's what I said. KICKED OUT!"

"You mean I really have to go?" I asked.

I didn't want to believe it. I couldn't believe it. Not with the road just inches away from its end.

"Couldn't I stay just one more week to finish the road?"

The lump was swelling in my throat, tears were sneaking to my eyes. I looked down toward Bari-Cotu, thought of Wally and the sobs broke.

"Oh shit," I sniveled. "I don't want to cry."

Archibald's fat hand pressed gently on my rib cage, his fat head leaned on my upper arm in comfort and his Stetson, which had only recently come out of mothballs, tickled my dripping chin.

"Ooooooooooo Yaaaaaaaah!" I moaned. "I don't want to go home. Th-th-th-thiiis is my home."

"Naw, honey," he said, patting and squeezing, "this ain't yer home. Specially now it ain't yer home."

I smelled his vainglorious after-shave, his breath mints, the mothballs and the acrid sweet whiffs of gin.

A crowd had gathered. No one could tell exactly what was going on except that it was bad and I was going to leave.

They followed me back to my house silently, respecting my sniffs and sobs. They watched me jam things into my old duffle bag. I took my few clothes, a toothbrush, soap, towel, and my emergency supply of glasses, Wally's telescope, my snapshots, a strip of embroidery that Alganesh made for me, hung my camera around my neck and walked with a stone face and a stone heart to the helicopter.

"I'll be back soon," I told everyone.

They were all there, as they had been when I arrived, staring at an awkward stranger who was trying to appear relaxed and not to stare back.

I shook each hand. Alganesh wept into the corner of her shawl and held her baby up in an attempt to reassure me that they would all be O.K. Even Tesfa, who had changed a lot, who, I knew, was glad to see me go, came up, did a few zick-zicks of the *iskistis,* to commemorate our night together, smiled and admitted reluctantly that what all the other Americans had done was not really my fault.

I could not admit this was goodbye.

I had to fold myself around that duffle into the luggage compartment of the copter. Several times I jabbed and bopped the poor pilot, who had pulled a black sweatshirt over his head and was attempting to sleep.

"Here's a little something to take yer mind off things," Archibald said, but I had no leverage, lodged as I was, and I couldn't hoist that big jug of Black and White, and there were no straws on board.

The pilot was yawning and swallowing coffee directly from the neck of his thermos. He fumbled and fumed and got it all going just as the first few drops of rain fell, mere whispers of things to come.

There was no window where I was, so I couldn't take long, lingering, aerial looks at Jiru. I could only imagine it, a ratty oblong of mud and thatch, stretching a long, new feeler out to the world that had ignored it.

What a misery I felt in that cramped and stifling quarter. Nothing seemed right. I wished I had never come to Jiru, though I couldn't think of my life if I had missed it. I didn't want Jiru to change in case I could come back, but I wanted more for those people, more food for one thing, a doctor and medicine for another, a better school, a better teacher.

I didn't know where I was going or how much time I had before I left. I could easily have worked myself up into a frenzy of misery, but there was something in that ride that comforted and soothed. My position was fetal and the roar made all talk impossible. I gazed through a triangle in the corner of my elbow, where a piece of metal had caught a glint of sun from somewhere. I caught the drowse and I did what I've been known to do when there's no bottle. I slept.

10. There were only a dozen peace corps volunteers left in the country

Besides me, there were now less than a dozen Peace Corps volunteers left in the country. Three of them were staying at the Princess Zikaye under what Tim Lomax was calling "house arrest" because of an eight to eight curfew.

It did not surprise me that Lomax would be one of the last to leave. He was the granddaddy of all volunteers, serving two years with the Camden New Jersey Baptist Missions and five years with the Peace Corps. He'd lived the whole time in a small village east of Jiru constructing a bridge over a river that had dried up in the drought. *Everyone* knew Tim Lomax. He was a Buckminster Fuller fan and had convinced the entire village to build geodesic domes. He was also a great believer in biogas, but he couldn't get that off the ground, because in hot dry climates, the shit just sits there and dehydrates. Once he siphoned some money out of Jack Archibald's purse to build a wind powered grain mill, but his windmill blew down every time there was a storm. He planted mulberry trees, hoping to develop a silk industry, but the worms got diseases and died.

Archibald called him the Minister of Wild and Woolly Ideas. Lomax had made a contract marriage with a beautiful whore, who retired from business to work for him raising mushrooms and garlic in the horse manure they collected from the stables of the local prince. Archibald called her the Ministeress of Fungus and Bad Breath.

Lomax was furious that someone was sending him home. "I cannot *deal* with it back there," he was telling Lee Ann Johnson, who had been assigned less than a year ago to teach tie dye in the women's prison. "I feel like selling this plane ticket," he told her, "and taking the Big Bus Ride. Ride buses right down to South Africa and then up the other side to Morocco. Take eight months, maybe a year, maybe forever. Put off the Big Return." He moaned into a cup of coffee.

"Sears Roebuck?" he said.

"McDonalds?" he said.

"Do you hear what I'm saying?"

He had the jet black hair of those Irish who had missed the gene for red, and the sparkling blue eyes of a leprechaun. His beard was enormous.

"No-no-no-no-no—" he shook all over, mimicking someone trying to get out of a full nelson.

"I know what you mean," said Lee Ann. "I don't really want to go home either. It isn't that I want to stay here though," she sighed. "It's just that I promised this guy I'd marry him when I got back. Now I'll never be able to get out of it."

"Maybe you could get reassigned someplace else," Max Mermelstein said. He was midway through an assignment with the Ministry of Rural Electrification, where he spent most of his time fixing the minister's radios. "I'm going to get reassigned to Barbados."

"And learn another language?" she whined. "I'd rather get married than do that."

"Anyway," Lomax said, "it says here they've closed the airport until further notice." He held up the newspaper which, like the phone in Adi-Duri, was coming free of charge these days, but getting thinner.

"It's raining in Jiffo," he said turning to the back page.

"It's raining in Adi-Duri—that's you," he told me.

"It's raining in Wello. It's raining like hell.

"Whaaaaat?" I moaned. I saw it all washing away, a river of mud. "What's going to happen to my road?"

"Pwooooosh!" Lomax answered. "Man, I just hope when that river starts up again, it goes *under* my bridge."

The paper next day said nothing, but the grapevine at the Zikaye said the country just below the mesas was having flash floods, the rain was washing off the bare hills and filling the valleys below. Someone reported Adi-Duri was underwater.

In the lobby I found Lomax eating guacamole, having bargained with a peddler for a small, but miraculous sack of avocados and conned the disbelieving chef at the Zikaye into mashing them up with a bit of onion and salt.

"I *can't* just sit here while everything is washing away," I told him.

He offered me a spoon and a corner of his bowl.

"My life," I told him, "is *washing away!*"

I really believed I had arrived at yet another rock bottom. It was only the sweet, oily, nutlike taste of the avocado that made me want to go on.

"If only I could find out that everyone is O.K.," I said. "Is that too much to ask?"

"Mno," he answered with his mouth full.

"Mno," I agreed. Oh, that avocado tasted good. Butter from the trees, it tasted of earth and sky, of grass and leaves and gentle rains. It ridiculed my misery. It damned me to enjoy myself.

"Mna," I muttered, "where did that guy get these avocados?"

"Mshurrrrrp," he answered. "I dunno."

After we had ravaged the sides of that bowl, I asked, "What would you think if I snuck off for a day or two and went up there?"

"You have a life raft?" he asked.

"It can't be that bad," I said. I refused to believe it. "The papers would have printed something if it were that bad. They'd have the UN in there."

"The papers are too busy printing news of the latest executions. Today they're wiping out the entire Ministry of Education." He grinned like a soldier in the Irish Republican Army who's just tossed a Molotov cocktail into a Protestant church. "You know, when I first got here, I worked for a slimy little bastard over in that ministry."

He licked his lips. Was it the avocado or the taste of revenge?

That afternoon Jack Archibald showed up at the hotel with a secret stash of Budweiser in a plaid suitcase.

"For heaven's sake," he bellowed up and down the lobby, "ain't nobody lookin' after you poor kids?"

Lomax winced, hid his face in his hands.

"Hey you, Shoulders over there, you got a thumb in your room to pull open a pop-top can?"

So we all trudged up to my room banging on doors until we had four of us and a one-eyed Jack, like the first hopeful poker hand in what turned out to be a long night.

Three or four hours later we looked like an entry for the word "sozzled" in the living dictionary. After we had finished the beer, Archibald opened his briefcase. What he had been calling his "Oklahoma lunch box." In it there were three bottles of Southern Comfort.

Lee Ann Johnson, who never tasted Southern Comfort before said, "Gee, this is real good. It doesn't taste anything like *real* whiskey," she giggled.

Archibald was busy telling her how she reminded him of his wife, Darlene, when Darlene was a little girl. "Oney I didn't know Darlene then," he said. "I wish I did. I wish I knew her THEN 'stead a NOW!" He walloped Lee Ann one across the back.

Mermelstein, wearing headphones, was plugged into a small cassette deck sipping a water glass full of Southern Comfort and listening to his only remaining tape—Jimi Hendrix. His eyes were crossed and his toes pointed in toward each other.

"He's short-circuited," Lomax said, cradling a bottle of Southern Comfort between his crossed legs. Long ago he had foregone a glass.

Archibald gazed with undying love on Lee Ann. "Naw," he said, "I swear that Darlene never WAS a little girl, but if she ever was a little girl, wha, she'd a been jest like you. Oney a little bigger in the chest," he slurred, tipped his eye for a closer look.

He leaned back to slug down some Comfort: an enormous silver belt buckle appeared from under his belly. It said "Hip Hip Hooray!" His zipper had opened and peeking from it was a bit of boxer shorts, pink with little blue butterflies.

"I know it ain't right," he said. "A man talkin' against his wife like that . . . ,"

He fumbled absently with his zipper: the butterflies fled. "Wha, I should be ashamed of myself. I AM ashamed of myself. Yes, I am. I sure am. But my heart's been broke and when a man's heart's been broke, wha . . . ,"

He lost what he wanted to say, scratched his head, looked pleadingly at Lee Ann, who, bombed beyond talking, answered "Hneeeh," and grinned. She was dabbing Southern Comfort behind her ears like perfume.

"Well," Archibald went on, "like I was saying, when a man's heart's broke he ain't a man anymore."

Tears filled his eyes. It was too much and he keeled into Lee Ann, knocking the poor thing to the floor. She rolled into Lomax and over on her back, puppy fashion with her arms and legs bent and in the air. Her shirt rose to her rib cage and her navel appeared like the center of the universe.

I moved in next to Archibald who was blubbering and mumbling about Darlene's navel. "I saw it once or twice in my day. Sweet as a rosebud. Yes it was."

I slipped in next to him and told him, "I've got to find out what is happening in Jiru." My tone was sober, even if I was not. "Just gimme your pilot and the helicopter for a few hours. Up and back," I said. My serious tone was slipping. "Puleeeeeeese," I slurred.

Oof, the foul Southern Comfort had formed itself like taffy into a sticky ball in my stomach where it was bouncing around bumping into nerve centers and sending the following message to my brain: "Will you get this Lulu to upchuck." The message had a sobering effect.

"Listen Sal," he said. "You jest better close that book," he said. "Wash your hands of it, burn that bridge behind you," he went on, mixing metaphors.

"Bridge?" said Lomax from the floor like a confused Buddha. He had been contemplating Lee Ann's navel.

"I was just telling ol' Sal here she better wash her hands and burn her bridges . . ."

"Puleeeeese," I begged. "Pretty please."

"Hush now," he said.

"Pretty puleeeeeeeeeese with sugar on top?"

"Oooooo, you're making me sick," Lee Ann moaned. She sat up, and covered her mouth with Lomax's hand.

"Not *my bridge . . . ,*" he said.

His eyes were trying to focus on the hand that covered Lee Ann's mouth, but before he realized that it was his own hand, her cheeks puffed out and uttering *"Yurp,"* she barfed all over him, sat back, started to cry and then yurped again.

Lomax yowled and started punching her. I leapt to the rescue pummeling the attacker. He reached back and socked at me, landing one on the bridge of my nose, thereby ejecting my shatterproof lenses, which flew like tiny frisbees across the room. His next punch landed in my eye.

I sank my teeth into the back of his neck mistaking it for his shoulder.

He reared up to throw me off, but I wrapped my legs around his middle and my arms around his neck.

"RIDE 'EM COWBOY!" Archibald shouted. "Whooopeeeee!"

"Wraaaaaaah," Lomax growled and, running backwards as fast as he could in that small room, knocked Mermelstein out of his chair and slammed me into the door.

I woke up next morning on the floor. Only one eye opened at all, a slit at best. Through it from my low vantage, the world was a realm of hazy foreign shapes cantilevering into my privacy uninvited. One shape was the bushy head of Tim Lomax between my legs, resembling John the Baptist's on a tray. I feared I had scissored it off during my attack, until I heard its asthmatic snore.

I carefully extracted myself, cradling that wobbly head from my thigh to the floor, and blundered my way through headache and miasma toward the duffle where my extra glasses, faithful retainers, waited without complaint. Thus bespectacled, my one remaining eye saw that Archibald was gone. It saw Lee Ann in the bed with Mermelstein curled at her feet still wearing his headphones. It saw empty beer cans and fallen glasses, the proverbial dead soldiers. It could have been the day after Hastings, after Agincourt, after Waterloo, Shiloh, Gettysburg. The day after the Tet Offensive. It saw a broken chair. A towel and a piece of newspaper had been hastily tossed on a pile of vomit. The smell of Southern Comfort vaporizing on everyone's breath and the various states of spill and decomposition were indescribable.

I tiptoed out of that shambles and down the hall to the shower. Terrified, I looked in the mirror. One eye was puffed with drink and the other was black and swollen shut. I pried both of them open with my fingers to get a better look.

"Gaaah!" I yelled. *"My nose!"* My nose was nowhere to be seen. Only its nostrils, hideously blackened with dried blood, remained, struggling to breathe. My poor nose had suffered *again*. I was finished, done, fit for nothing but the part of an extra in a cheap horror film.

In the shower, icy water from the hot water tap beating on my throbbing head, I wished I could be reincarnated, yes-yes, as the first woman ambassadress to Mars where, because of my great earthly beauty (no wallops or shiners), I would mate like crazy and start a new race. I was fed up with Earth. It either provided no water or too much water. No food or too much food. Its diseases were vile and rampant and its people not much better. I was fed up with the whole race. It scrapped and stank and as if to add insult to injury, it demanded perfection of itself so it could always fall short and end up slobbering with regret and feeling sorry for itself.

Oh what's the use, I bubbled and blew into the shower. My stomach heaved and rumbled. I belched and farted. What a spectacle! It was fortunate that no one was around to witness.

Far below me I saw my feet. I had forgotten to take off my tennis shoes. Their laces floated sadly on the water which had backed up, was up to my ankles and threatening to spill out of the stall. I wanted to take a swallow of whatever it was Alice had taken to get small, so I could be sucked away on an eddy, down the drain to proceed unnoticed toward the place where the sewers go. There was, alas, no way to disappear.

Naturally, I was not the only one in such a state that morning. I met Lee Ann in the hall as she rushed toward the toilet, this time with her own hand on her mouth. And in the room itself Lomax had climbed onto the bed in her place and covered his head with the pillow.

"All I want is coffee," he was saying. "And my toothbrush."

Lifting the pillow and then slamming it down, Lomax said "And an aspirin."

Mermelstein, miraculously recovered, offered to go to the bar and get some coffee.

"And my wife," Lomax said. "And a beer."

"O.K., Lomax," Mermelstein said as he left.

"And my mother," Lomax said. He pulled the pillow off completely, saw me and started to laugh.

I bellowed, "Don't look at me! I haven't got my makeup on yet."

"Did I do that?" he asked.

"It was self-defense," I admitted. I was trying to tie my soggy sneakers to the small railing of a six inch wide balcony. They dangled over the street. Big drops of sludgy water fell from them like acid rain.

"Do you feel as bad as you look?" he asked.

"If I ever felt as bad as I looked, I'd have to kill myself," I answered.

"You want some of this?" He had found an unopened can of beer among the rubbish and was popping its top.

"Hair of the dog?" I declined.

"Piss." Lomax complained, and blew the beer like a tanked up whale. "I'm sorry but this shit tastes like piss. American beer. What're they making it with these days? P.I.S.S."

He shot another spout and then another and it looked like so much fun, I joined him, grabbed the can and *psspitewie!* contributed to the alcoholic mist that, together with the stench of last night's Southern Comfort, was rendering the room unlivable.

"Shit!" Lomax said suddenly. "I'm *not* going to let them send me home."

He propped himself on his elbow. I could see the black tufts of a very hairy chest at the neck of his T-shirt.

"Look at it this way," he reasoned. "Peace Corps gave me a ticket which I don't want, right? Now, there are *lots* of people out there who want tickets, but don't have them. The Greeks, the Italians, the Lebanese, all those business men the junta isn't going to let out of the country until they've paid up for ripping off the masses. What do you think they'd pay for my ticket?"

"Nothing," I answered. "Your name's on it. You know, Lomax, it's not like a subway token."

"What if someone used my name?" he asked.

"Sell your passport?" I gasped.

"Yeah," he mused.

It sounded more dangerous to me than a drug deal. "It would never work. No one is getting out of here on your passport but you."

"So what if they don't get out," Lomax went on. "No skin off my ass."

"How would you get out then?" I asked.

"I'm not getting out, dummy! That's the point," he said.

"You might change your mind and want to get out." I was sounding for all the world like a killjoy.

"Then I would simply report my passport stolen," he answered. "Believe me, it's doable. Look, I've even had an offer."

"Who?"

"Johnny Mamalingis."

Mamalingis ran a Middle Eastern restaurant, a butchery, a bookstore and a garage.

"Mamalingis says if he grew a beard and his hair, he'd look enough like me to get out on that passport. You want to know what he offered me for it?"

"Don't tell me."

"Would you believe fifty grand in local currency. I'm only talking about the passport, we never even got around to what I'd charge for that plane ticket."

"What are you going to do with all that local currency?"

"I'm going to *live here*. I've got a wife here. I've got certain things going. Once I'm on that plane, I'll never get back in. They're going to close this place off. Like China."

"I'm sick of China," I said.

The whole thing was making me very sad. I didn't want to leave either, but there was no Greek out there who could grow a beard and end up looking like me.

Mermelstein returned with the coffee and a message that the airport was being opened, and Americans had been given three days to get out.

The news made me nearly as frantic as Lomax who was swearing and pacing and trying to figure out whether he should sell his passport and ticket, dreaming up scenarios, what-would-happen-ifs, alternative approaches. I paced as well. Mermelstein told us to relax. But we couldn't. As soon as the curfew lifted, we both rushed out. Lomax didn't say anything but I had an inkling he was going to find Mamalingis. I ran like Mercury to the nearest post office where there was a pay phone.

I dialed. The phone hesitated on the ring, stammered, and then burst into life. "*This phone is bugged so look out what you all say!*" it said.

"Hello, Mr. Archibald?"

"Issat you Sadie? You got a big head?" he asked.

"Remember, last night," I lied, knowing he couldn't possibly remember last night, "you promised to lend me your whirlybird for a quick up-and-back to Jiru."

"Listen, Sugar," he said. "No one holds a man to a promise he makes when he's eating an Oklahoma lunch."

"But how am I going to find out what's happening in Jiru? We have to leave day after tomorrow."

"That's right and it ain't too soon for me," he said. "Now you quit worryin' about Jiru. Everybody's jest fine out there, jest like they always been." He hung up.

I dialed again.

"I AIN'T LISSENIN,'" he bellowed this time.

"I'll pay for the gas. I'll pay mileage. I'll reimburse you for the pilot's time."

"You think them reds are gonna let all you persona non gratas fly around this country peekin' and lookin'? You want to find out what's happened to Jiru, you better come have a look at a satellite picture over at my office. Wha, them bastards'll shoot down that machine soon as they see it go off the ground."

"No they won't," I said. "Not if we take off at dawn. No one will see anything."

"Maybe not," he said.

He kept the helicopter in the American Embassy compound where it would be able to sneak away unnoticed.

"Well I can't agree to it 'less that pilot a mine, ol' Gary, agrees." I heard a beer can pop open.

"Call and ask him. I'll call back."

I was jumping up and down. My wet sneakers sucked and squished. I gave Archibald ten minutes during which time a dwarf waiter from the tea shop across the way came up, asked me to go dancing with him—*iskistis,* he hissed—and giggled away like fury.

I dialed. Nothing could have meant more to me at that moment.

"Jest remember," Archibald hollered through the receiver. "It wadn't my idea."

"Then it's O.K.! Tomorrow? Crack of dawn? Embassy compound? I'll be there."

"That's right," he chuckled, "But ain't you forgetting 'bout the curfew, gal? Curfew's made to keep people like you from gittin' away in the dark."

I had to risk it.

It was only about a half a mile from the Princess Zikaye to the embassy compound. The Zikaye was built along the top edge of a ridge, like everything else on that street, with its back facing a steep gorge. Narrow paths and ditches wound down to a putrid stream along which hordes of squatters crowded in shacks made of cardboard and wood scraps. The ridge itself ran up to a big Coptic church on the eastern side on one of the city's main squares. Through some woods and across a narrow street was the British church, St. Andrew's, then more woods, some shops and a garage belonging to Johnny Mamalingis. The garage abutted a large school compound, and then more woods followed a sloping road up to the American Embassy.

I figured I could make my way up there without having to step out into the street where the soldiers patroled. Besides, according to the conventional wisdom of thieves, early morning was the time when the guards slept the deepest, when the first pale light told them their watches were over and they could relax.

11. I grew painfully aware of my privilege and the guilt that goes with it

Next morning at 5:30, carrying Wally's telescope for better views, I climbed out the bathroom window and down the rickety, wooden back balconies of the Princess Zikaye. I could hear people in the kitchen running water and starting cook fires. Someone above me pulled a toilet chain and then, below me, a pipe spat the flush into a stinking ditch that wandered towards the squatters below.

I walked along the ledge behind more hotels, restaurants and apartment buildings, afraid of dogs though there were only cats, thousands of wiry cats with chewed up ears who, like the birds twelve hours before them, were selecting perches for their off-hours. The air smelled of cat piss, ordure, and the camphor of burning eucalyptus breakfast fires. It was easy, a nice morning stroll, though my heart was pounding and popping, and the pits behind my knees, which weren't receiving any blood, were shivering.

I climbed easily into the church compound over a stone wall and followed it, behind some friendly shrubs, to the northwest corner where, with some difficulty, I scrambled up and jumped down onto the road. I knew right away that I had not found my metier. I was out of control.

I hopped across the road like a scared cricket and pushed through a hedge, not without some blood shed, into St. Andrew's. I crossed behind the church itself, pressed, ouching, through another hedge and slithered through the woods. I could see the backs of the shops. A few security lights revealed piles of empty cardboard boxes.

There was a loading platform behind the butcher shop, a small, asphalt parking lot and then a long wooden fence that ran the length of the complex ending at Johnny Mamalingis's garage, the back of which was littered with cars in various states of disrepair.

It was just beginning to get light. I ducked behind the fence and skidded along its length, the space between the slats clicking. The gray morning light was like a strobe. Through the last slat I saw the soldiers. One was sitting on a chair between the garage and a fruit stand, and the other, wrapped in white homespun, was asleep in the fruit vendor's cart, his gun propped against the rear wheel.

I had to get past the dead cars somehow and under a wire fence into the school yard.

The soldier on the chair appeared to be asleep as well: I could see his head nod forward and then loll to the side. I chanced a quick dash, landed next to a flattened red Fiat, said a silent prayer for whoever its driver had been, and dashed again, landing this time between a Peugeot station wagon with no wheels and a Land Rover with no roof. I was crawling happily down the corridor between these two fallen heroes, knees and elbows bleating in pain, when suddenly a rifle dropped across my path. There was a third soldier. One I hadn't seen.

I opened my mouth to scream, but my everlasting throat lump was there, this time in fear, blocking everything but a weak and rasping "Yeerghk" as I stuck my head under the Peugeot's front end like a compromised ostrich, waiting for that gun butt to whack my butt.

Nothing happened.

I waited.

Still nothing.

I pulled my head out. The gun was still there, fallen from in front of the Land Rover and now propped against the Peugeot's bumper.

I peered under the Land Rover and saw the other soldier's feet. Immobile. He had been asleep too, only now he stirred. His feet scuffed here and there in confusion, then they crossed as he reached (I could hear a yawn and I could see an arm) to pull the rifle back to his side.

I had to back down that dreadful corridor, which now seemed as long and threatening as the Khyber Pass, but I somehow made it, reconnoitered and tiptoed to the shelter of a line of VW Beetles behind which I crouched my way to the school, went under the fence on my belly and was up and running on the other side, legs like pistons, breath like a broken cylinder missing every other stroke.

I huffed and chugged across a soccer field, behind some lavatories, behind the main classroom building and out the other side into the woods that took me to the embassy gate.

The guard had been told to expect me. A conspirator, he had the gate open as soon as I popped from the trees into his view. "Good morning," he said as though everything were perfectly normal.

"Good morning," I answered, dusting off my clothes. Vainglory. The knees had ripped out of my jeans, the elbows of my sweater were frayed, a smudge of orange decorated my middle and my toes poked out from my shredded, soaking tennis shoes. God knows what he thought of my mug, the purple shiner, the swollen nose, the bloody scratches I had acquired taking this morning constitutional. But the old guy took it in his stride and continued with a long string of greetings and salutations which I thought would never end.

Archibald's pilot, Gary, was there drinking coffee from his eternal thermos.

"Get in," he said.

He looked at me in wonder. "You really got Archibald wrapped around your little finger," he grumbled.

"I remind him of his wife," I said.

"No shit! So do I!" he answered.

"Wha, you sure do remahnd me of Darlene if oney Darlene was a man!" he drawled. "But that Darlene ain't no MAN I'll tell ya!!!"

He checked his equipment, fired the engines, spun the helicopter's propellers and we lifted, tipped and sneaked out of town.

I glanced down the hill toward Mamalingis's shops and saw

from the air the soldiers, still asleep, one like a sack of papayas in the cart and the other like a showroom dummy in the chair. The third, who had given me palpitations had risen, turned, and flopped belly down on the hood of the topless Land Rover.

We circled and flew north. Away from the road, we traveled over small poor villages. The round thatched houses were grim, black dots in the ancient ruined landscape, like punctuation marks in a prophesy of doom. We flew over the first crow's feet cracks of Africa's great rift, over one gorge so deep it had its floor in the tropics, a jungle full of vines and malaria. We passed the big towns like Makele to the east, so no one would see us. Then as we turned and made our way toward Adi-Duri, we began to see evidence of the floods.

I began to wish I hadn't come.

The rain had filled all the low places. Towns were abandoned, their poorer sections washed away. Water lapped at the sides of buildings that had withstood it, poured through the open doors and low windows. Tangles of clothes and broken furniture caught against signposts and stranded cars. Here and there strange bloated shapes floated. I hated to think what they were. My heart thickened and my spirit plummeted. I knew there was nothing I could do to help down there except run back and make a report that no one would listen to. I was only there to spy, to peer and snoop, to satisfy my curiosity. Airborne, literate, healthy, possessor of a plane ticket to the land of plenty, I grew painfully aware of my privilege and the guilt that goes with it.

As we dawdled over that sad countryside, I felt a strange thrill. It was like the thrill I had felt when I first looked down on that foreign land and saw those round thatched houses, the geometries of their compounds and fields, the wide stretches of a green I had never seen before and a sky clearer than I had ever been under. The volunteer who sat next to me on the plane had whispered, "Look, that's *Africa* down there!" There were no roads, no cities, no airports, no oil refineries. There was no Jersey Turnpike. It was all wild, I had thought then, full of strange plants, weird animals, untamed. But I had been wrong. It was full of people. They were only hiding in its tired valleys and in the hopeless shelter of its ruined hills. This time, saying goodbye instead of hello, I was thrilled, not by its newness but by its familiarity, by my intimacy with what was down there. I felt the way I imagined a person might feel when she chanced to meet up with an old lover, one who had asked *her* to leave, one that she still loved. I felt embarrassed, complicated, a little wary—a lightening in the stomach and a quickening in the heart. Thrilled.

The marketplace in Adi-Duri had become a small lake. Nomads were camping on its shores as though it had always been there. The streets of the town were still rivers, but here and there people were starting to come out; their clothes and linens flew from poles like flags in the bright wind. Every flat rooftop had women on it tending the wet clothes, hefting and turning heavy mattresses, spreading grain and vegetables in the sun. When they heard us coming they broke from their work, stood, looked toward the sound, and waved like reeds feeling the river's current.

The business of repair is always more serious than the business of routine. They paused only a few seconds to rise and watch as we circled and passed. Their bodies were beautiful, as confident as dancers', because, as any Kansan knows, when you start putting your wet potatoes in the sun, you only do it because you know the worst is over.

Unlike Pompeii, Bari-Cotu had not been preserved forever by the disaster. No one was still sitting there, fork full of spaghetti in midair, poised, ear cocked, face frozen, in one split second of clairvoyant recognition that something terrible was about to happen. Bari-Cotu looked as though it had made a pathetic attempt to build a barricade along the western rim of the town. I peered through Wally's telescope toward Bari-Cotu once again. Once again the premonition. I hesitated. The small brass chain was cold on my cheek. The mud houses had pitched into their own rank alleys and narrow streets. Window frames and door frames. Cupboards, tables, chairs. Broken.

A few of the buildings stood. Wally Martin's old house was one. After Wally had died, the owner moved back in. He was there, the only person I saw in Bari-Cotu that day, alone, just standing in front of the porch craning to see the approaching aircraft as though he thought it might be coming to help. I recognized him right away. He was wearing Wally's bright orange sou'wester, bare legs under it like bent cane.

I shouted a greeting to him, leaned out, waving and shrieking. He smiled and waved.

"Is everyone all right," I bellowed, but, of course, he couldn't hear a word I said. My attempts at sign language only caused more smiling and waving. The situation was not conducive to charades.

Even from there, and even as preoccupied as I was, I could see that the road to Jiru had not survived the flood. Along the recent memory of its way, a troupe of Bleeding Hearts loped and dallied. I had an inkling they had just helped themselves to the soggy grain stores of Bari-Cotu. A few huge males jumped up onto rocks and watched us approach. Their wives and children fanned out in all directions, paused, found friends or parents and looked up with languid interest at the noisy machine that hovered over them in the sky.

I was full of grave inklings and palpitations as we approached Jiru. What I had forgotten, of course, was that Jiru, my little hilltop Jiru, isolated and miserable as it was, was on the high ground.

"It's still there!" I shouted.

Yes, yes, I saw a slight crumbling at the outskirts. The hilltop itself had grown more peaked and confined as the edges of Jiru had eroded. The odd storage bin and the odd outhouse had slipped away. The road had slid off sure enough. Its drains and culverts were revealed as the foolish attempts they were. But the essential Jiru was still there. I counted its houses as its folks, stirred by an old familiar sound, rushed out.

What in all creation could be closer and yet farther away than to be hovering over your loved ones of the moment, hovering over your whole world in a coughing, whirring helicopter being flown by a callous bastard who won't land. All I could do was shout and wave. All they could do was shout and wave. Most of Bari-Cotu was there.

"Can't you get closer!" I shouted. But Gary was as close as he would go.

"Is everyone O.K.?" I bellowed.

I wondered what I had been thinking of, coming out all this way without bringing anything, not even a newspaper so they could know what was going on. I remembered the Americans dropping chocolates all over Europe at the end of the Second

World War, not much help, a silly thing to do in the face of that devastation, but what the hell, I would have done a silly thing like that. I *wanted* to do a silly thing like that, only I had no chocolates. The only thing in that helicopter was Gary's thermos full of coffee. Half full by now. God, in retrospect it's a wonder I had the forbearance not to dump that hot coffee over everyone, for want of any other silly and fleeting gesture of love. Instead, with much pain, but no real second thoughts, I tossed out Wally's antique telescope. The message I intended to leave with that dear instrument was that I would be back to get it.

"Satisfied everything's alright?" Gary yelled.

I nodded, crying and straining for my last looks.

As the helicopter lifted, everyone down there realized sadly that we were not going to land, that we had come for mysterious, foreign reasons which it wasn't their business to know or try to understand. To them it must have seemed rude, a greeting with no handshake, no warm touch, no kisses, one on each cheek. Only Alganesh seemed to understand why I had come: she lifted her baby high in the air like a banner, to reassure me that everything was O.K.

Jiru dwindled below us then as Gary bent his flight path, arching toward the north and east. We followed the road along a flat stretch that sloped upwards toward a distant climax and then dropped, out of the clouds, down an incredible escarpment to the sea. There were no cars on that road. The countryside seemed totally abandoned. The only evidence of human life was that the hides had been stripped from the dead cattle that rotted along the road, so many of them that even the vultures and hyenas had a hard time keeping up.

We left the road and had just started south on our way back when I saw the first geodesic domes. I shouted "Stop! Wait!"

"Wait?" Gary yelled. "Are you shitting me?"

"There . . ." I saw another cluster of domes and an angry river out of its bed rushing helter-skelter through the domes like fingers grabbing at spilled pearls. Lomax's bridge was tossed among them, high on the only bit of dry land there was. A road to nowhere and a bridge over nothing. It made me laugh.

I laughed and laughed. I laughed until my bladder begged me to stop. "Oh, look!" I burbled and choked. "That bridge . . . ," and the two of us howled then because we both saw there was no end to the ridiculousness of white men and their amazing schemes.

12. Mermelstein suggested one last walk downtown

I worried all the way back to the capital about breaking the news to Lomax that the river had by-passed his bridge. At least, I thought, the bridge was still there, more than I could say about my road. But Lomax was not at the Zikaye when I returned. Curfew came and went and he still had not shown. I began to suspect that we would never see him again. I began to suspect that he really was the Minister of Wild and Woolly Ideas, though on the other hand Mermelstein suggested he was the Minister of Golden Opportunities and had just taken one. Lomax had been talking to Mermelstein about Mamalingis as well.

It was less than twelve hours until anybody traveling on an American passport had to be out of the country. What a depressing thought. Even as I sipped slowly at a sublime papaya shake, delicately flavored with the juice of sweet limes, I could only think that this was my last taste of that wonderful, fresh and flowery drink. I felt like a journeywoman on Olympus taking her last sip of nectar, a melancholy reminder of mortal connections. I remembered the Zarex and Kool-Ade of my youth. That papaya might have been the juice of a pomegranate, sentencing me as it did to a Hades of tasteless sweetenings, frozen and thawed essences, and artificial flavoring. It's no fun to be banished. I felt constricted, freedoms compromised, options gone. I felt falsely accused, betrayed, dished out a punishment I hadn't deserved. Furthermore, I had no idea how it happened. I wasn't even sure *what* had happened.

Mermelstein suggested one last walk downtown. It was a slow meander. We poked around our favorite spots, picking listlessly at the city like kids who have been in the cookie jar all afternoon pick at Saturday night supper. Everything I saw, felt and tasted, tried to tell me that I was still the same and the place I picked and poked at was still the same. But it wasn't.

It was on that walk that I realized that words can disrupt the hearts of humans as quickly as famines and floods can disrupt their bodies and ruin their homes. There was a big square—the Square of the True Cross—at the far end of town. It remained empty of buildings, its entrance marked by a towering arch, the signature of a tyrant, a place reserved in which to display his armies, to stage his celebrations, to make his grand speeches. Now that the tyrant was gone, his square was being used for public executions.

The morning paper printed the names and positions of those men and women who had been sentenced to be executed that day. Mermelstein was curious. He had had a short flirtation with SDS and some vague Weathermen connections while he was in college. Killing off corrupt politicians and evil decadent royalty (*cf.*, rich industrialists and oil men) had only been talk then, words. He never thought he would get a chance to see it happen. I don't know how he did it—maybe some fast talking—but Mermelstein convinced me to accompany him to the Square of the True Cross.

The executions were in progress. Sometimes they went on all day. We had heard the firing squads even as we left the Zikaye. The crowd was enormous. I had seen this crowd before: every year at the annual celebration of the True Cross. When the emperor and his lions appeared traveling the long route through the city to a high platform at the head of his square, that crowd had fallen to its knees in worship. It had wept, overwhelmed by love for him. Torches and bonfires filled the huge space, and a veil of smoke made the King of Kings seem distant, deep blue in color, like Krishna, light years away. His armies rode horseback or marched, goosestepping in front of him and his people. His ministers and his barons flanked him, princes from all over the country. Now his army held him prisoner and was killing his ministers and his princes, and his crowd was cheering, high on words that were promising them a better life and telling them here was the retribution they had always wanted though they had not known it. Telling them they had been had for centuries. So they erupted, half-starved, on the last of the last adrenalin their glands could pump out. And it was no wonder. It was no wonder. But I didn't like it.

There was a sick atmosphere of festivity. Someone was selling balloons to the kids. I had a horrible sinking feeling that I had helped set him up in business.

"Let's get out of here." I yanked at Mermelstein's elbow.

"Not yet." Mermelstein was entranced.

An execution had just taken place. Three bodies lay crumpled at one end of a long cordoned-off section of what was now

Revolutionary Square—no longer the Square of the True Cross. Those heaped up but unmistakable forms were just visible to me over and between the heads of that mob. If only I had been a foot shorter, better yet, two feet shorter, I wouldn't have been able to look over those heads. God knows I didn't *want* to look.

"Listen Mermelstein, I'm getting out of here."

But I didn't budge. It was a case of what Plato described as appetite over reason, the same thing that makes even the squeamish peer at grisly automobile accidents and buy tickets to freak shows.

I sensed a break in the activities. A strange quiet. I could smell incense. Revolutionary students were hauling off the dead with the casual lack of ceremony of trash collectors, alternating between macho display and light banter. A collection of army officers sat in relaxed positions in front of a long table on what was formerly the imperial dais and was now the people's platform. Banners bearing revolutionary slogans and pictures of the struggling masses had replaced royal portraits and symbols. A few of the officers climbed down and a few more climbed up. They milled around on the stage discussing among themselves. Two waiters in white jackets brought up trays with teapots and cups.

"Tea!" I gasped in the direction of Mermelstein. I felt ill. Even he paled, turned quickly away and looked at his newspaper—the list of the damned.

"They're going after a bunch of petty princes today," he said lightly. "For crimes against the people."

The crowd was very quiet now, waiting. The waiters carried off the empty tea cups and the officers settled into their places at the long table, shuffling papers and blowing into microphones, all signs that the next group of prisoners was about to be brought up before the people, where their names and crimes would be read and their sentences pronounced.

Three names were shouted into the microphone, scratchy and barely recognizable with the volume. It was only after a few seconds that I realized one of those rasped and doomed names was Zerahun! The pits behind my knees suddenly filled with ice water. I drew my breath in shock and found, when I went to breathe out, that a terror lump was pressing on my esophagus, blocking my exhalation. Acid poured from my heart into my stomach.

"Oh no," I whispered. I grabbed at Mermelstein. "But he had escaped. He had gone. Out of the country . . . no, no, no," I babbled like a maniac.

I'll never know how, but I dared to look. I prepared myself, felt suddenly calm, though I noticed that my legs had crossed, and I was standing on my own foot, one heel driving into the other arch. When I looked up I saw an old man, perhaps Zerahun's father. His head was bent, his face in shadow.

"I'm going," I told Mermelstein. "You can stay if you want." This time reason took over. My curiosity was dead.

"Detach yourself," Mermelstein said. "Think of all the deaths those bastards have caused."

I detached myself alright. I began pushing my way through that crowd. It was packed so tightly by now that I could barely move. I pulled against it with my arms, swimming. More than once my feet came off the ground in the jam. I couldn't get out fast enough. Behind me the microphones pounded out the crimes of Zerahun, the names of the children of his tenant farmers who died of hunger, the money he stole from the country to keep in Swiss banks and to send his sons to schools abroad, the women he had violated, the bribes.

I slumped free at the edge of the crowd, exhausted and weeping, sitting on a rock. Two little girls held hands and stared. They were ragged and barefoot and their noses were caked with snot. They never flinched at the sound of the rifles that fired all at once into Zerahun. One of the girls was wearing an ancient apron. It hung below the frazzle of her dress. I could still see the remains of a gay print, hens and flowers. The pockets, one of which hung loose and flapping, were egg shaped. She reached into the other pocket, found a filthy handkerchief and offered it to me. I knew at a glance that handkerchief could qualify for the *Guinness Book of Records* as the filthiest one in the world, but I used it anyway. It smelled of wood smoke and cow dung.

I decided to go back to the Zikaye and close my eyes for the rest of the day. I had seen enough. I had seen too much.

Somehow I managed to sleep. I slept and slept and woke up only because Lee Ann Johnson was banging on my door telling me it was time to go.

I emerged surly and puffed with sleep that I didn't need. I was grumpy and sour when I saw Mermelstein, who looked slightly guilty, like a kid who'd gotten caught masturbating. He said he was certainly glad to be leaving. Lee Ann nodded. She was fidgeting with her passport and health cards. In her wallet she found a picture of the kid she had to go home and marry.

"What do you think?" she asked me. "Cute? Actually he's even better looking. This is a bad picture." She sighed.

I sat down, closed my eyes and leaned against the back of the chair. I smelled charcoal fires and boiling meat from the Zikaye's kitchen. I smelled the strong coffee left in someone's cup in front of me. I smelled the sweat left on my own body from the morning, and I wished I had showered. It was going to be a very long night.

I kept my eyes closed in the cab that took us to the airport. I tried to think of when or if I had said goodbye, in my heart at least, and then I thought that I hadn't, and then I thought that I didn't want to.

At the airport there was a rumor that a wealthy Greek was trying to skip the country, traveling on a forged passport and disguised as a Peace Corps volunteer. The junta, a sort of male-collective version of the Red Queen in *Alice in Wonderland,* wanted to cut off everyone else's head. The rumor was that we were all about to be thrown in jail until the imposter was revealed. It was only a rumor. The jails were full. We could see easily that we were on our way out. They had a special flight arranged for us, a special customs check and a special room, empty, ignominious, nothing in it but a fluorescent bulb.

Jack Archibald was in the customs line ahead of me with his wife's six Siamese cats in three small cages. The customs people, revolutionary soldiers who had replaced corrupt bureaucrats, had never seen Siamese cats before and thought Archibald was smuggling out a rare and endangered species. They were not going to let the cats through. When we walked in, there was Archibald with his arms raised like a holdup victim.

"Might's well shoot me down dead as let me on that plane without them cats." He leaned, cronylike, into one of the young soldiers. "Listen, I'd jest as soon let them cats out right here and now. Wha, then we'd see who was the endangered species!"

He winked and guffawed and slapped backs and the soldiers, who didn't understand a single word, stared back as though they wished there had never been a revolution and they could simply go back to their barracks.

"Lemme tell you 'bout this one here."

Archibald started pointing at one of the cages, but seeing the approach of his friends and drinking buddies, he broke off and started whaling backs and shaking hands, suggesting that we all go on upstairs and find a bar while the soldiers sorted out the problem with the cats.

"One a them cats," he said, "is Darlene's mother come back to life." He chortled. "Oney she ain't dead yet!"

He was wearing an old, faded Dixie T-shirt that said "FORGIT HELL!" and he positively reeked of hooch. No attempts at a cover-up. He was starting to develop a dowager's hump.

"Ooooooooooo, I HATE them cats," he growled. He displayed scratched and bitten arms.

"Here's Darlene goin' out the door." He stuck out his chest, cocked his head to one side, then in a husky female voice said, "Honey, you can bring the cats. I'm going on ahead to do a little shopping in Paris."

He dropped the imitation of Darlene and imitated himself. "Wha Darlene, sugar, you KNOW I CAIN'T even pack mah own socks. How'm I gonna pack them CATS."

I noticed there were even some scratches on his neck.

"Them cats like to ah killed me."

Inside the bright room reserved for us, a few officers from the new government talked to a handful of American Embassy officials. They seemed curiously congenial under the circumstances. Denver Cox from the Peace Corps was there greeting us, counting us and asking if there happened to be anyone who knew where Tim Lomax was. Some airport immigration records showed that a certain Thomas Lomax had left the country on the first flight out the day they opened the airport.

"He *always* did things his own way," Cox grumbled, when it became clear that Lomax was not among us that night.

Stuck as we all were in that room, like quarantined victims of a rare disease, we were forced to listen to the parting comments from the embassy spokesman, a type my uncle Eddie always called a wiener, "scraps, filler and preservatives in an artificial casing." He talked vigorously about how such inconsequential differences should never stand in the way of a renewed and productive friendship between two countries that had a fine history of firm and friendly cooperation. What a headache I developed listening to that claptrap. I was nothing but a headache.

Claustrophobia is not normally one of my many problems, but that night I had a very bad case, a wide-ranging claustrophobia. It wasn't just that lunatic asylum of an airport that I wanted to be out of. I wanted to be *out. Out. Out. Out.* I thought of immediately applying for astronaut training where at least I had the hope of getting stuck in an orbit around Jupiter. That morning at the execution, I had been horrified to be a human being. That night I was ashamed. Perhaps the entire race ought to be locked up: one half in jail and the other half in the loony bin.

Instinct told me that that wiener of a spokesman was blowing a great chance to say something about that famine and those floods in the north that no one was doing anything about. He was already kicked out (the diplomat's dreaded destiny), but he had zero balls.

Those are *not my* parting comments I wanted to shout. That spokesman is *not* speaking for me. It might have been a perfect time for *me* to strip. It was the end, a time when words were being shorn of their meanings.

Wally had said, "A famine is not in the eye of the beholder, a famine is not in the words and statistics of the reporters, a famine is not like the sound of a lone tree falling in a huge forest. It's only the people who have enough food that think so."

There was no doubt that this was not a good way to end my career in the Peace Corps. I had no idea what it all meant—Wally, Zerahun, Alganesh, Tesfa, the children in Jiru (kids, who now knew about Bartholomew and his wonderful hats), the whores in Makele, the old phone man in Adi-Duri, the bleeding heart baboons, my tiny house where Wally was so sick, our road, my mesas . . . oh, I was sinking, poor heart breaking. Nothing was finished. Not even the road.

But all at once, yes-yes, that road twinkled up out of that dark reverie. It sparkled and danced to life on a note of imagination as golden as if it were made of yellow bricks and going to Oz. Tee-hee-hee, my sinking heart chuckled from within. Ha ha ha ha! As I walked through that cold night to the waiting plane, I fancied I could see that road under my own clomping and ragged tennis shoes, and I knew that Zerahun had escaped along its smooth surfaces and that during the whole of last year when there was hardly any food at all in that valley, no one in Jiru had felt more than the smallest pangs of real hunger, and I bowed a bow and winked a wink for that road and for Wally and for me. It hadn't been a road to nowhere.

BACK BAY TO THE BUNDU

Every day before she took the lunch Cook had scraped together down to That-Man-Stan, Frances Eliot worked on her memoirs. "Back Bay to the Bundu" was her running title.

She wrote propped in her ancestral bed. It filled the end of her one-room house like a great ship in a tiny harbor. It was a bed, Frances said, carved by some wag in order to turn the theme of its marital purpose inside out. The headboard, in deep relief, pictured Daphne changing into a tree, foiling the randy Apollo in graphically hot pursuit. Across the top of the footboard a row of fat-cheeked cupids stood pissing, as it were, on the mattress. Gargoyles and devils popped out of the high posters. Even someone like Frances, who was shucking off possessions, could not have left such a thing behind in Boston, where it might have ended up in an estate sale.

"I'm packing with my tongue firmly in my cheek," she told her nieces, who loved the thought of having an old, fat, eccentric spinster auntie living off in darkest Africa. "Taking only the most necessary nonessentials"—bits of heirloom silver, her mother's pearls, crystal candlesticks, the Sargent portrait of her grandparents, the little Winslow Homer watercolor, and the bed, of course. Everyone else in the family was furious and tried to have her declared non-compos because she had cashed in this and that and made a nonsense of one of their sacrosanct trust funds.

"It's one of the oldest, most primitive impulses in man," she told the nieces as she emptied out her trunks and closets into their waiting arms, "to go off and die in the wilderness." The arthritis in her hip was so bad, she said, and her bones were so big that she hurt twice as much as anyone else her age. The end could not come soon enough, she said. And so on.

Going off to the wilderness to die was the main theme around which she developed her reasons for leaving. Hadn't she watched her own father, old as Methuselah and ready to go, being rescued again and again from the jaws of death while she and everyone else stood around saying, "Not me. Don't ever let this happen to me. Not with all those tubes." Then it dawned on her that he, too, made such requests, all of which were roundly ignored, even as he screamed out into the corridors of Mass. General, "Call off the ghouls!" Cars from chase scenes poured out of a TV mounted on the ceiling. "The monsters! The monsters!" he went on shouting. He was already in hell as far as Frances could see. She told the hospital, using language she reserved strategically for such times, to take the mother-fucking television thing down and let the old man die. She was glad for her height and flesh then, as she brushed nurses aside like so many flies.

Later, when she announced her plans to emigrate to Kenya, she told the family, "I know that, at my age, the only way I can be saved from doctors is to go someplace where there aren't any." Then came the hearty laugh she had developed when she was a girl at Vassar, playing the Red Queen in an avant-garde production of "Through the Looking Glass."

At other times, weaving a theme around the advantages she had had all her life, she declared that she was sick of being so everlastingly comfortable. Her life has been exciting, yes—a series of grand tours starting in India when she was ten, punctuated by periods in Boston when, as a girl, she attended boarding schools and, as an adult, she did what the childless wealthy were expected to do, sponsor civilization and help the poor. She said that she wanted to go live humbly in a remote, wild place. "Among lions and nomads," she liked to say.

Her family paid no attention to any of the reasons they extracted from her, because they attributed everything she did to an overblown nature and failed ambitions on the stage. In fact, she confessed to her nieces, *they* were the reason she was leaving. "To get away from their everlasting, everlastingness."

It was on one of her grand tours that she had first come to Kenya and met Stanley. His last name was Polish, which she dismissed immediately as unpronounceable, christening him That-Man-Stan. He was originally from Boston himself, a coincidence they got monumentally schnockered around for the several nights spent in Nairobi. It caused a terrible scandal in the tour group because she kept going off with him and coming back in an opera-buffa condition—she huge and afloat in her floppy trousers and stained blouse, and he all skin and bones in pants gathered by an old string.

Stanley had been detailed to Kenya during the Second World War to fight Germans in the battle for the Bundu and he never went home. Some British settler conned him into buying a derelict piece of property by daring to call it a ranch: eight hundred acres of semiarid Bundu onto which Stanley put two hundred head of European beef cattle that he sold as steaks to whites in the capital.

It was a good business for a long time, but on the night Frances met Stanley, he was just about to go bellyup with only forty head left, and these looked rather more like the indigenous zebu cattle than Herefords, with big humps and big horns and very little in the steak department. On a lark, Stanley offered Frances a full partnership in the ranch at a price to be fixed later, explaining that he could restock the place and make a fortune.

The crowd of scurrilous Brits who drank at the Norfolk Hotel in Nairobi warned Frances not to do it. The ranch was a farce, they said. Stanley had gone completely bush. He lived in a shack so run-down and terrible that even his African woman refused to live in it. He had hired a bunch of Borana ranch hands to keep the Masai from stealing his cattle, but the Borana, with no thought whatsoever for the laws of civilization, had simply moved in and overrun the place, grazing their own cattle on Stanley's pasture—such as it was—and mating their miserable bulls with Stanley's heifers.

"Oh, who cares?" Frances roared. Certainly she didn't care.

She went out to see the ranch with Stanley who, quite sober, was driving around in his ancient Land Rover. Even his appalling house had a certain value, showed how little one truly needs, hinted at some ordeal of purification. The land was dry, claiming its riches only from the colors of earth—layers of rusts and ochre. Even the sky that day was washed a faint sepia. Trees were burnt scribbles along the edges of empty riverbeds, and the wadis' thick black scars dragged through the dust. She loved it there. In the northern section there were huge boulders that could have been clouds turned to rock and fallen from the sky.

She imagined the Borana had stories about the boulders, myths, legends. But Stanley said no. He had no explanation from geology, and no curiosity either. So she joined it all, accepting the great rocks as evidence of things that could not be understood, an appealing idea one can come to late in life and not lose balance.

Images returned to her—the Himalayas, the long valley of Kashmir turning violet and purple before a storm, the river Jhelum (or was it Ganges) down below, a silver wire twisted around jade forest. She saw all of China rising tier on tier until it made a dome, a tiny opening of sky into which she would evaporate. As if she were drowning and her life were passing in front of her, she tried to understand at last what messages, if any, could be given in the language of such haunting landscapes. They stood on a ridge and could see down each slope, into the whole world, it seemed. "I will build a house right here," she said, "with windows on both sides."

Later, in Boston, she attempted to translate the feeling into words by talking about Olduvai—"Why not take your last footsteps in the place where mankind took his first"—sounding unfortunately like a travel brochure or whoever it was that had stepped down on the moon.

Her Maragoli cook, whom she called Cook in her Red Queen voice, brought cup after cup of the best coffee as she scribbled on the memoir, strewing papers like rose petals in some pagan festival. But the deuced thing was impossible to write. She was compelled to start over each day with a new idea, so she never got past the first chapter, sometimes entitled, "Fire in Ipswich: The Childhood Years," referring to a fire that almost destroyed the family's summer house on the salt marshes. She was nearly lost to it, glowing in her bedroom closet, hidden in anticipation, waiting for something to be revealed. She intended, in the chapter, to discuss the story of youthful defiance against the destiny determined by her ancestry. But she couldn't find any form. There was some parallel she felt between her own spirit and the fire that had turned the house to ash (not exactly ash: timbers marked out a ghostly frame, the chimneys remained); it had to do with the way the firemen had pulled her out and given her back to her father, like being captured and turned over to an enemy. Thinking of it—her life enclosed between the fire and where she sat writing now—in terms of composition, she was suddenly inspired by the concept of parenthetical expression.

"I have lived my life in parentheses!" she enunciated. She tossed a sheet of paper. She was not exactly sure what she meant. She tried another version. "I *am* a parenthetical expression!" She was practicing for lunch with That-Man-Stan. She would swoop down and enclose him as well. She inhaled. Air filled her lungs and seemed to lift her, like a balloon, against the pain of stiffened joints. She was roused. Her house was perched as if on the rim of the world. She had survived the flood. Through the banks of windows looking out both sides, Africa offered continually dramatic views. In this way she felt diverted by each small moment, especially in the morning, with a herd of zebra just inches away. "Cook!" she shouted. She was floating, but she still needed a little help getting out of bed.

As a neo-rancher, Frances cultivated an image. She bought an old pickup, a relic christened Queen Victoria, which she got in and out of with some difficulty but drove fiercely, like an ambulance, administering first aid to the Borana who lived on the ranch. She deliberately looked like hell with her baggy trousers and sweaters full of holes. Her luxury was not to care. She had cropped her hair and come out domed, rather like Gertrude Stein. She thought it uproariously funny that her cook had the pinched looks of Alice B. Toklas; instead of making hashish fudge, he dumped local gin into everything. They needed the empty bottles to store water, he said. This caused confusion when it came to making gin-and-tonics at sundown, until Frances got the idea of hanging her mother's pearls over the real thing.

She liked the scene she made each day, roaring out in her truck to look for Stanley. She might find him down near the north well with some of his Borana herdsmen, watching a newborn calf. She was often struck by how perfectly ridiculous he looked (he was bowed in the legs and getting worse) and drove up on a long laugh, raucous enough to meet his chortles. Lord, how his teeth had gone yellow. She could have wept.

"If it ain't Miss Fran." He had some kind of Texas accent that he usually put on at lunch. ("Wha, ah'm ready to eat a dad-blast horse if ever a man was born.") He came along to help her get out of the pickup, sniffing for the lunch which she knew was dismal because she hadn't gone shopping for a month. It was boiled meat wrapped in a bit of cloth.

Oh, still it was delicious to sit near the well where a few trees had struggled and survived, gnawing on the salty, stringy meat and drinking beer. Drinking, actually, rather a lot of beer so that she dozed and woke up in confusion, looking, as always, for something that was receding into the distances all around. Into the emptiness.

"Stanley . . ." There were so many things she wanted to say, in a serious way. Time, quite clearly, was running out.

He was looking at her. He could have been one of the cattle himself, big brown eyes, an innocent lope, despite the fact that he was sitting down, and in the act of swallowing.

"Last night," he said, "hyena chased down a sheep. BLAST!"

"Last night I had a dream . . ." she said. In fact, there was no dream. She was going to make one up to tangle Stanley: he looked so small, half his size, even pumped up full of beer that way.

"Yeah, a dream?" His legs were wires holding his feet on. She realized she had never seen his feet: it made her miserable.

"I dreamed . . ." But there she was without any dream, stranded. "It's actually a recurring dream," she lied, "in a very big house that is growing bigger all the time." She could hear him breathing and she could smell his smell, tobacco, cow shit, never mind.

"I need tell my men a thing or two," he was saying, ignoring the false dream; then he started talking to his headman, a Borana he called Tonto. He seemed to speak their language, but Frances was never sure. All the giggling the Borana women did whenever Stanley opened his mouth indicated that he was making mincemeat of it. And if it wasn't outright disobedience, then it must have been ignorance that caused them to ignore his simplest instructions.

"Does he understand what you just said? I doubt it," she grumbled, to challenge the image he played up as a macho, although a bit arthritic, Kenya cowboy.

"You can only trust a Boran so far," he admitted. He thought they were devils incarnate, second only to the Masai, a hook on which he hung his grudging admiration. The more they stole from him, the more he liked them—bloody bastards—continually pitching his own wit against them in losing battles. But if he won and caught the buggers rustling his cattle—well, then it was the triumph of the century and he would gather the Borana all around into something like a court that no one took seriously. Then they slaughtered a bullock and had a feast.

For the rest of the afternoon, Frances and Stanley drove around checking on the stock and the condition of the pastures, such as they were. Near the east boundary there was a rock with a gentle configuration that allowed Frances to climb up its left bank. She called it Lion Lookout—not terribly original, but yes, you mostly saw a lion if you stood up there. This was where the two of them usually ended the day, with a thermos of hot tea prepared by Cook and, if they were lucky, a packet of fried chicken legs that tasted rather like the pickup by then.

That day they could see Borana gathering in what Frances called Sunset Ravine, a wadi that filled up with red and orange lights as the day went down. They were shadows marked by the edges of their white cloths and the black slashes of guns across shoulders. They were stencilled forms that looked like lettering. She never got tired of all the things they were. A gathering of clans no doubt. A few camels had arrived—a festival? From the ridge where her house stood she had often looked down on their fires like phosphorescence in the grass. In bed she could feel them alive and moving in the dark, drums that had no fixed place, calling.

"They're at it again," Stanley said. "I'm sure that pain-in-the-ass Tonto will be off tomorrow hustling my cattle on over to his brother's place." Because cattle, it was known, had been created expressly and exclusively for them and sometimes had to be reclaimed—including Stanley's, half of which belonged to Frances. She and Stanley leaned shoulder to shoulder on the rock, contemplating the gall of Borana.

But when they went down there to see what was going on, they found that a child was missing, a girl who had a Masai name, Nolomai. Frances became a riot of concern. She piled warriors and women into the back of the pickup and tore off to search, grinding the gears. They broke into parties, fetching Stanley's Land Rover, as well as warning Cook. They searched until the bitterest dark, along the wadis, fearing lions. There were cascades of stars, dry bushes falling from the sky over the windshield. Cows were flying. Frances forgot about her arthritis as she jumped in and out of her pickup and, with searchers flanked out on either side, walked, almost blind, calling "Nolomai." She knew she was berserk. When it seemed impossible to go on, she watched for Stanley's lights along a track and went to meet him.

"Nothing," he said. "We'll go back out in the morning."

Borana had surrounded the two cars and were still intense. A delegation waited in the back of the pickup ready to escort Frances home or simply to go on riding fast, exalted by the dark night—anybody's passion.

"Are you coming up to my place?" Frances asked Stanley.

"Sure," he said. "We'll be able to see what's going on." Stanley hovered like a U.F.O., possibly thinking of gin and maybe food up at Frances' place.

As they approached her house, a small light on the ridge growing brighter, they saw Cook running, waving an old rag.

"She is here!" he was shouting. "She is here. The lost girl."

He had brought out a chair and allowed her to sit. She was

about ten. Easily the first time in her life on a chair, she had it all wrong, was perched with the weight on her feet, ready to topple. When she saw Frances, she stood. Like a statue. Like a Giacometti, Frances was thinking, all angles, her feet and hands exaggerated. Her face, however, defied any sort of comparison, as if it were black crystal, or black cut glass. Her head was shaved. She was naked but for a tiny leather apron covered with colored beads.

Cook was chattering the most insane nonsense, "A white man," he pulled at Frances and Stanley. "She says a white man is bring her." He ran around. His words were like ribbons, drawing them in, tying and wrapping.

"Oh, yes, certainly, a white man," Frances laughed. Stanley was the only white man for a hundred kilometres.

"Yessssndio," he hissed, combining languages. "I am say no." He shook his head. He had never trusted the Borana and vice versa. He was one of those Maragoli from Kakamega, the sort that became crooks, the sort the Borana had no use for. "A white man?" So Cook was having a laugh too. "A lie, sure."

"Ask her again," Stanley said.

There was a flurry of languages. Stanley said something but there were no answers, only giggles until the girl finally spoke. And then there was silence. A party of Borana had followed the commotion up to the ridge and now stood watching, shifting quietly. Cook was pressing close to the girl, but looking at Frances and saying, "*Bwak, Bwak,*" like a chicken.

Cook was bonkers; Frances had always known.

Frances took charge. "Ask her what this *mzungu* looked like. Was he tall? Was he short? Was he fat? Was he thin?"

Stanley tried asking, but the girl wouldn't answer, tipped her head away.

"You see!" cried Cook. "There is no *mzungu.* She is trying to break into the house and steal." According to him, the sole occupation of Borana.

"Well, ask her where he went, then," Frances insisted.

"Yes, where . . ." Cook began, and translated in a threatening tone.

The girl spoke softly, her voice amazed. She opened her arms like wings and lifted them, then lifted her head up and back, lifted her body, too, up on her toes. Frances saw now that she was marvellous.

Stanley asked her something. Again she rose, up, up, said something in her voice, whatever the words were. The whole thing had silenced Cook.

"She says," Stanley reported, "that after he brought her to the house, he told her to stay here and then he lifted his arms and went up."

"Went up?" Frances repeated.

"Up." It was difficult to tell what Stanley thought, if anything.

"Really, Stanley . . ."

"I didn't say it."

"Ask her again what he looked like. What he was wearing."

Stanley hunkered so he was looking right at the girl. Cook held the lantern close. The child positively glowed. They talked. He looked up at Frances. "She doesn't know," he said, "but no trousers. A cape maybe, a *shuka* is what she says. No shoes."

Cook was laughing nervously. "A white man in a *shuka?* With no shoes? Flying up?"

"His face. What was his face like?" Frances asked. A wild image was forming. "Was there a light shining on his face?"

"What kind of stupid questions . . ." Stanley said.

"Ask it!" The Red Queen voice pushed out.

Stanley asked. The girl was nodding. She was smiling at Frances.

"Yes, a light . . ." Stanley said. "But she says what she thinks you want her to: it's an ole Boran trick, the rotters." He was extricating himself, trying to stand up, and his bones creaked.

"A djinn," Cook said. "A *shetani.* Yes, it is true." He was quite frightened now.

"A *shetani* would have eaten her, for God's sake," Frances said.

"Later, it will be eat," Cook said. He suddenly remembered something: "An owl bird. I have seen." According to him, this was a terrible sign: he threw stones at owls. "Two owl birds." Soon it would be three, then a flock, Frances thought.

"Sounds like Jesus." Frances snorted. She had a fantastic suspicion that, indeed, it was a miracle that had happened, even though she had been raised an atheist. She had the sensation that she possessed something. Was it the girl? Or was it the girl's bizarre hallucination itself that was being given to her this way, delivered to her doorstep as a test? Or something even more astonishing, like those boulders, that would allow no explanation?

"No, never!" Cook, who had been baptized, after all, a Seventh-Day Adventist, bowed his head. "Borans people can never see Jesus, the Lord!" he declared.

"Oh, why ever not?" Frances was irritated and wanted to be alone with the child. "Nolomai. Nolomai." She bent, coaxed, offered a hand. And the girl swayed.

"How can Jesus . . . ?" Cook was frantic, wringing his cloth, trying to enlist Stanley.

"Admit it, Stanley," Frances said, laughing. "Exactly like the ascension." She lifted her arms; her large bosom rose.

Stanley was either gagging or laughing. "You never know

what a Borana will tell a person," he said, dragging out, she thought, another of his tiresome Borana clichés.

Cook was a severe annoyance, almost crying, "Memsab—all of us—down in the hell fire."

"Nonsense!" she bellowed. The child was shining in the meager lantern light.

The Borana were simply standing around. Professional at waiting, they had settled, bringing all their life with them, regardless of the hour. Women were nursing. Kids were dragging sticks around. Dogs were lining up to screw.

"Who are the parents of Nolomai?" Frances asked. The reaction was classic: no one would admit to anything. Cook's shoulders slumped. The Borana shifted, a few of the women stopped nursing.

"Nobody is parents," Cook said.

"Hopeless," Stanley whispered.

"Tell them that Nolomai will be staying with me for a few days." Up until now she had no idea what she might do, though she knew she had to do something. She still was unclear, had no instincts that applied to such situations, only this voice telling her to keep the child. The child had been delivered to her door. She instructed Cook to explain this to whichever person out there was in charge, offering a hundred shillings for the girl.

Cook walked forth, a sad figure, and returned an equally sad figure. "They say you never put her inside this car. Because in this car you will take her far away, maybe Nairobi, maybe New York."

"No car," Frances swore.

"This one will be wait to watch you." He pointed to one of the women.

"We will not leave the premises," Frances promised. She was

obsessed now. Oh, if only she had been such a child, led by a vision away from the lions in the night—well then, who, who indeed would she have become? She saw that she was nothing, the confirmation of her worst suspicion.

"Come, Nolomai," she said gently, and the girl, without looking back, walked to the house with her.

Inside the house, all the next day, she talked to Nolomai, whose name could have been wind blowing over the tops of boulders. She began to take down all of her nonessentials from the crude shelves Cook had installed—the silver, the crystal, old books, jewelry. Splinters from the brittle wood stabbed her hands.

"This and this and this—all for you, Nolomai." She went on talking about everything as Nolomai listened, her eyes round, pupils like jet. Her lashes were long as the swirls of Arabic script.

Nolomai appeared to know she had been chosen and sat relaxed, as any proper goddess ought to do, waiting to be delivered to her fate, or to deliver others to theirs. The old woman thought they were both being twisted together in order to find out something at the same time. Easy, then, to drop at the child's feet all the worldly goods of Frances Eliot, her last will and testament.

"All of these things are for you, Nolomai . . ."

So glorious because the things, in absolute fact, were pure and had no value at all. She could see the silver pot in a tarnished future, covered with the soot of Borana fires. And the little Winslow Homer, which Nolomai was viewing upside down.

By nightfall the girl was weary and wanted to go, but Frances wouldn't let her. Cook brought them roasted goat while Frances lit all the candles she had so that they would be dazzling on the ridge, a cosmic sign.

Cook sputtered, "But, but, for wasting why? All your light."

Frances was hopeful that the apparition of the night before would return but didn't know how to make it happen. The candles seemed as good an idea as any. Perhaps there had to be terror and the threat of a lion for it to appear.

She began again to tell Nolomai about the gifts that were still laid out on the floor, kneeling among them in front of the child goddess. There were people who knew what you had to offer, and if there was nothing concrete left, there were insubstantial things—what you knew, or didn't know. Nolomai, who had remained placid, like a fetish, rose, put her hands on the old woman's head, as if to draw something from her; as if the memoir would be formed against everything Frances had ever done to prevent it.

"It was an empty life," Frances confessed. Then she wept and the girl absolved her.

Cook, endlessly nosy, would not let such horror continue. He called the Borana in to take Nolomai away from the kneeling, crazy memsab whose face was startlingly white. Frances tried to protest, but she was weak and being stabbed to death in her hip. Was it broken? Seized up like an old engine. Did it matter now?

Next day, though stiff, and worn down by emotion, she faced Stanley at lunch with a bottle of gin and the liver of the roasted goat.

"I knew they'd take her. I knew they wouldn't let me keep her," she told him. She was in a fit of crying. "She was like a daughter to me." It sounded rather absurd, she knew, but she wanted to tell him.

"A daughter to you? Whatever you say, old girl," Stanley put his arm around Frances and ogled. There were things that he had no capacity to understand, like truth.

Still, he was what she had, an awful choice—no choice, in fact. We will die together like two old marrieds, she fantasized, though we have both avoided that—wanted to avoid it—all our lives. Oh, yes, she longed to see his feet, or to touch the spotty old hand that was perilously close.

THE BLONDE MASAI

O. K. I was willing to overlook it when this Alex from Chicago showed up with so much camera gear that I had to put my backpack on the roof rack. He had a retainer from *National Geographic,* and, Lord knows, I didn't. But when he said, "What I really want, for my own collection, are shots of animals, you know, going at it," I thought, oh God, no. By then it was too late. We were already approaching Namanga on the border between Kenya and Tanzania, hoping we had all the necessary documents to get across—car permits, visas, health cards, currency declarations.

I'd met Kurt, Nancy and Alex in Nairobi at the New Stanley Hotel. They were going to Tanzania and looking for one more to help pay for gas. I was on my way home after two years in the Peace Corps training nurses in western Kenya and had decided that I wouldn't leave East Africa until I'd seen the Ngorongoro Crater. This was not so much a fixation as it was dues, the kind you settle on when mildly intoxicated by staring at maps and listening for two years to peoples' stories of strange places they're headed for. As in: I'm not going home until I go up and see those gorillas in Rwanda. Or climb Kili. Or whatever. I liked the word Ngorongoro-ngorongorogoro, like drums or echoes, and I liked the idea that this was the holy place of the Masai, a people who made you believe they were the only experts in these matters.

When she saw me, Nancy said, "Like it'll be nice to have another female in the group." She was from Rhode Island and had been traveling almost a year.

Kurt was from Salt Lake City. He wore his auburn hair in a thick braid that he doubled back and wrapped in a leather thong. Good looking, with dark eyes and thick black lashes. He was very pale though, an achievement on the equator. It was his car, an old Peugeot station wagon that he'd bought in London, and he did all the driving. He listened to Cat Stevens tapes the whole time, through headphones, so when you sat behind him it was as if the music were coming out his pores, familiar as sweat. He did this, I realized right away, because he hated to talk. *Moon shadow, moon shadow.* He had met Nancy in Athens a few months before. I figured they were lovers. They had picked up Alex in Cairo.

"Just a couple days ago," Alex was saying, "in Samburu Park, lions. You ever see cats do it? They keep at it for hours. I even left for lunch and came back. Right, Nance?

"Oh, gross!" she said without looking, from the front seat.

"Hyenas," he said in my direction. "Just like dogs."

"He's some kind of weirdo," Nancy assured me.

"Hyenas are hermaphroditic," I said, immediately regretting it.

Of course, he knew. "The female," he told Nancy, "has this false pecker." He prodded her shoulder.

"Yeughk," she said and covered her face.

At Namanga we drank beer on the veranda of an old hotel. In a stone lined pit there were some tortoises mating as if they had known Alex was coming. He had antennae for such events, drawn somehow by the expressions of the crowd that had gathered, and he waved us over. "You gotta see this!"

There were several Masai warriors, Morani, positioned so tourists could photograph them for a price. This always made me sad even though I knew there was an unpleasant presumption in that emotion having to do with believing in noble savages, a nineteenth century affliction. They were just looking for some cash to buy tobacco or snuff, maybe sunglasses. Of course, they all thought the turtle business was hilarious and Alex even more hilarious down there in the pen with his camera.

Nancy had said, "Oh God, I can't stand the way civilization is spoiling these beautiful people," which made me wonder what she thought of herself. As for Kurt, he was too intensely austere to be above suspicion. What you detected in him was a fearful desire for luxury which in people like the Masai is set free—their lavish vanity, their posing, the rumors of sexual abandon, their chauvinistic god. He had acted, too deliberately, as if they weren't there at all, these wild men covered in beads, smeared with ochre, long plaits of hair hanging to their waists.

As we drove into Tanzania, I waited for the landscape to to tell me something, but it was veiled, gauzy and muted. There were no edges, no features. You forgot the sky, even the road. The car seemed to float. You could imagine you were looking down from on high, scanning the earth. Nancy had her finger on a map—"We should be right near it. We should be falling into it." Alex was asleep. The light rose in waves from radiant pasture, lifted forms from it and snatched them away—shadowy cattle around a water hole, Masai maidens like rocks suddenly brought to life, a spell lifted, rising from the ground to fan out and wave to us as we passed, all smiles and elaborate structures of beads.

We stopped in a small town to ask directions to the Forest Lodge, a low budget place known to tourists like us. It had been a private house once, owned by a white family who raised cattle. After independence they lost their land but kept the house, added rooms to it, and tried to stay on as a hotel. Finally the government took that from them. The road to the lodge dropped as the land formed steppes to the south. In the distance to the northwest, the land built, improbably, what looked like a wall of trees, a mass of gray-toned jade. Beyond that, according to Nancy's map, was the famous crater.

We saw a man on the road, dressed in a shirt and trousers. His walk gave him away as white even before we got close, and Kurt stopped to offer a lift. He was middle-aged, heavy and drenched with sweat. He smiled and waved us on saying he was just out getting some exercise as if it were some suburban street in North Jersey.

"I mean isn't it dangerous? Aren't there *lions?*" Nancy asked.

Alex laughed and started to fiddle with the light meter. "Well, you nev . . . ," he started but lost his thought clicking and clicking the small instrument at the window.

We saw the man later at the lodge where there was a lawn set with tables for afternoon tea. He was talking to some Masai women who had wandered in and were trying to sell milk gourds by placing them on the ground in a row and standing silently behind them at a distance—prescribed, no doubt, by the hotel management—so you didn't quite know what they wanted. Nancy was certain they had come to beg for water or "something like that." Kurt, however, suddenly appeared in front of them and it became clear by the way they placed the goods in his hands that they were in business.

"I think I'll go check it out," Nancy said. I sipped tepid, bitter tea. The sugar was on a plate, crude brownish lumps that attracted bees. These swarmed, making a terrible racket, but they were passive; you could put your hand into them and take the sugar, letting them walk over your knuckles, dance between your fingers.

Kurt, more than the others, intrigued me. I invented things about him. Salt Lake City: he was probably a Mormon. I knew little about Mormons except the usual stuff: an angel called Moroni, two men, Joseph Smith and Brigham Young, some disappearing tablets and the miraculous sea gulls that ate the locust plague. I knew they were fundamentalists, forbidden alcohol and cigarettes, but that the men were allowed many wives. I remembered young Mormon men dressed in dark suits coming to our door when I was a kid, wanting to testify, and my mother, a Catholic, listening and nodding, and finally shaking her head in disbelief when they left. And I had a friend in college, Linda, whose mother had been a Mormon and who talked about rebellion in terms of fierce pain, in terms of deep scars cut into the whole family, and though I never got all the details of the story—a runaway, a trip on foot across the desert, release that came in Mexico in Yucatan, a pyramid, huge, glowing flowers and some wild idea about God—more than once I lay awake wondering about the woman. It wasn't hard now to translate those images and see Kurt.

Nancy came back with a gourd, a beautiful thing, stained deep red with the ochre Masai paint. It was in a leather sling stitched with blue and white beads and capped with a wooden peg. The neck was long and slender. The body was full. She carried it like a piece of the finest china.

"I paid thirteen shillings for it. I probably got took, but it's only a buck." She sighed and took back the gourd. "That old guy speaks Masai," she told me.

His name was Sanders and he was American.

At dinner he introduced himself and his wife who was carrying a book big enough to be the collected works of Dostoyevsky. She was small, the fingers on her left hand stained with nicotine. She had thick gray hair and weird amber eyes, a color I have never seen before or since. When she sat down she put the book next to her plate and tapped at it restlessly like an angry kid who's been told she can't read at table. They talked the whole time but in low voices; he mostly, in the tones of someone talking to himself, weaving theories or planning day trips.

Our first course was what my Peace Corps friends in East Africa called "corn starch soup," making the old joke about a chicken that walked through it. Only this one, on the menu, was listed as cream of mushroom. Kurt left it after turning his plate a few times and studying it from different angles. Alex emptied the pepper shaker into his. Nancy announced that she would eat anything, which was pretty much the way I felt about it. The second course was listed as zebra steak but no one really believed it. Boiled cabbage. Boiled potatoes. It was the kind of food you pay strict attention to, searching for flavor.

Mr. Sanders leaned over. "It really is zebra steak," he said.

"That does it. I can't eat it," Nancy said and she pushed the meat away. Alex stabbed it with his fork. It tasted like beef to me.

We were served coffee in a big living room in front of a fire. I was sunk in a deep shabby sofa. Kurt, seated on the floor, was a geometry of negative space, the light from the fire behind him pouring through the angles of his arms and legs. I was aware that he was our focus: Nancy, Alex and I were staring at him. Mr. and Mrs. Sanders stayed in the dining room where they had been joined by some local men. A waiter passed us carrying beer to them, after he had told us that there was none. When Alex complained, the waiter looked at him and grinned. So we left, carrying flashlights through the dark to our rooms, sending light streaks into the pitch black of night. Our voices, too, like searching beams.

Because of chronic water shortages, they had disconnected the plumbing in our rooms and dug pit latrines. Normally in such cases, I would take to the bushes, but that night, maybe because it was still early and people were still about, I took my flashlight and went down wrapped in a blanket against the cold. They had built a tall wooden fence around the latrine: men to one side, women to the other. Just beyond the fence was a barrier of plants, tall wiry succulents that had woven themselves together as they grew. Bare like cactus and watery green, tangles of thin stems. Someone or something was there, an antelope or a zebra grazing at night; or something smaller, a red-eyed genet cat or a wild dog. But when I shined my light at it, there was Kurt, naked, facing me. Slowly I traced his body with the flash. He was as beautiful as I had imagined, thin, well-formed, almost flawless except that his left side—shoulder, chest, hip—was slightly smaller than his right. At that moment the defect seemed significant, an explanation. It filled me with intense pleasure as though we had made love.

"Ooops—excuse me." I seemed to take forever to speak.

He laughed. "It's O.K.," he said and passed next to me on his way back to his room. In the morning when I woke up, I wondered if it had been a vivid dream.

We had to be at the crater's edge by 8:00 because only government Land Rovers could take tourists down. They left in the morning, returning at noon, one round trip each day. Kurt was waiting for us at the car with his elbows on the roof. He had the windows open and was playing his Cat Stevens tape. He had somehow managed to get himself clean with the soup tin of water that was delivered to the room along with the morning tea. At least he looked clean. Perhaps he had only changed his clothes, brushed and rebraided his hair. The rest of us looked dirty and tired even before we started.

Alex came up behind me saying, "There's supposed to be a shitload of rhino down there. Rhino!" I wondered if he was thinking of his private collection.

"I'm soooooooo excited," Nancy said.

Mr. Sanders was there and asked if we were going to the crater. He wondered if he could have a ride to the entrance with us. From there, he said, he was going for a walk.

Kurt told him yes.

"A walk?" Nancy mouthed in my direction.

In the back seat next to her, Mr. Sanders talked about the Masai. The wind and the Cat Stevens made it impossible to hear him, only the phrase, "twentieth century" which he repeated several times, like doom, in counterpoint to the lyrics "Will you tell us when to live, will you tell us when to die."

In a lull, Alex turned to him and asked if there was any way he might be able to photograph the Masai in their "intimate" surroundings. That word made me nervous.

"You can't just go in there and take pictures of them like

they're freaks or something," Nancy said. "You've got to live with them, get them to trust you."

"Oh, that isn't easy to do," Mr. Sanders said. He smiled as if he were condescending. "Even in the simplest things, there is a great mystery to their lives. For almost ten years I've been plotting the movements of certain family groups, but I still don't know much."

Nancy looked at him in awe waiting to hear more on the subject, but he became silent, smiling gently, staring out the window.

A view of the crater was flickering through the trees. For a moment, as the road came close to the rim, I glimpsed the great cup, steaming with gray-green mist, and in the parting haze, saw the hint of emerald forests and plains below. Ahead at the park entrance, we saw the small fleet of Land Rovers and tourists standing around, cameras and field glasses hung over their necks.

There were Masai warriors posing for pictures near a signpost and a bunch of women and girls selling gourds and necklaces. Old men and children sat on the steps of the park office. They all knew Mr. Sanders. It looked as though three of them had been waiting there for him, a young boy and two old men, bald as stones, whose earlobes, pierced and stretched, dangled sadly at their sunken cheeks. As we bought our tickets to join the tour, I watched him leave with his companions, talking earnestly. One of the old men was holding his hand.

Kurt and Alex were sent off in one direction, Nancy and I in another, herded with two British women into a waiting Land Rover. The women wondered why they were doing this. "My stomach's been off since Madrid," one of them said bitterly. She wore a funny little kerchief tied under her chin and moaned as we came through the low bush and started down the narrow dirt track we could see hugging the cliffs below, "Down there?"

The other cars ahead of us dropped in jerks as if they were being lowered on strings. A cloud hovered at eye level for a long time which made it seem that we were not descending but zigging back and forth, like fools. The crater appeared to be shallow but we never got closer to the bottom. We craned toward it.

"It's like going back in time," Nancy breathed. Suddenly the car paused and when we looked, we were there.

Where was the sun? At the bottom of the crater we lost shadows and all direction. The horizon was overhead, its edges pulled out in a long flat oval of sky. I imagined wind—pale streamers tied and rippling from end to end, except that it was still, not a breeze. Everything looked carved in marble and fixed in place. Lions posed, on a knoll or draped over fallen trees. Rhino, white, against a steely background, hyena fixed as if walking in a frieze.

Nancy, perhaps trying to visualize some distant past, had closed her eyes and was sighing, straining out the window, blind, as if her other senses were somehow better, less vulnerable to distraction. It was a good idea. I tried it and it worked. When I opened my eyes for a split second, in the blur the monstrous cars appeared like prehistoric animals shrouded in mist, grazing slowly toward extinction.

I heard Nancy say, "I wish I could come here on foot and sleep out. I mean worship here like the Masai do. Watch the sun rise and set. See the baby rhino being born."

"You sound rather like my husband," the dyspeptic woman said. "But you should hear him when there's no hot water at the hotel." We all laughed. She handed her camera to me then and said, "Do you mind? I always manage to get my thumb in the picture."

"It's like a temple," Nancy sighed. I felt the heat then and the stiffness in my limbs, the sadness of a broken spell.

Back at the top, Alex complained that everything was too artificial, like a zoo. He had actually fallen asleep near the hippo pools, he said. Kurt seemed pleased, even dreamy, talking in a low musical voice to the drivers and to the other tourists. He bought some stuff from the women there: earrings, an elaborate bracelet, and a bone snuffbox on a brass chain.

We found a gang of overlanders at the lodge setting up a camp on the front lawn. They had come in a truck with bits of their itinerary written on the side: London, Istanbul, Jedda, Addis Abeba, Nairobi. They looked as exhausted and filthy as their gear, about twenty of them, bickering over who was going to do the chores this time, in a patter of British and American accents.

I heard a tall girl tell a guy with a beard, "I'm one hundred per cent disillusioned with Ernest Hemingway. You can lean out the window of the truck and pull an elephant by the tail," she said in a loud voice. "White hunter? Just another silly bragging American."

"Hippies," one of the waiters whispered at the evening meal.

The kitchen killed a few goats and managed to produce some beer. It seemed like a party—the noise, the stories.

After dinner, we gathered in the living room again near the fire. An American called Wink, one of the leaders of the group, told me, "We're going down to the Cape and then up the other side. This is my third time." He *loved* Africa. "In Jo-berg half these babies will bail out. Maybe ten of us will make it back to London. Maybe less."

He was with a very yellow-looking kid who was obviously battling hepatitis and losing but who had a beer anyway. "How much is ivory down here?" he wanted to know. "I'm buying ivory. Like it was *cheap* in Zaire."

People were still filtering in from the dining room when Mr. Sanders suddenly interrupted, tapping a bottle with a spoon to get everyone's attention. "Please," he called out, "I want to take the opportunity of having you all together here to make a small inquiry." His back was to the fire. Mrs. Sanders had come in with him. Her book fell open on her lap, her head bent, automatically, into it.

"I understand you people have come from the northwest, isn't that so?" Mr. Sanders asked. Some nodded, others shifted in their seats and looked bewildered as if they either didn't know where they had been or as if they thought this man was dangerous. "I'm seeking information regarding a missing person. A young man. Twenty-five years of age. He will be quite tall and has very light, really blond, wavy hair. He was seen in the area you have just traveled through five years ago, dressed as a Masai warrior. I have a picture of him taken by some people in a group similar to yours. It's not a clear picture, but you can see, unmistakably, a white man there in the crowd." He held up a small black and white snapshot. "I also have this picture taken when he was fifteen, at the time of his disappearance, which I will be glad to pass around. His mother and I thought that, perhaps, as you stopped in markets and villages, you might have seen or even heard of him. He was seen near the crater two years ago." He passed the pictures around.

"Kid must've been grabbed or something," the ivory fancier said.

"Nope," Wink answered. "They were missionaries here and the kid ran away. I know the guy who took that picture."

Mr. Sanders stood near the fire, smiling, as the pictures moved through the crowd, a candid shot of a lanky boy carrying a backpack, the promise of a handsome man on his face, and another of a pale figure in profile surrounded by men; the long blond hair, the leather cloak, partly obscured in the dust.

Missionaries? Ironic, that it was their kid who had been converted instead of the other way around. Or was it something else, some way of taunting all of us who believed in an identity imposed at birth? Not an ordinary runaway, this boy seemed a link to what our yearning was all about.

"Do you think he's dead?" It was Nancy behind me. "Like I have a creepy feeling."

Wink shook his head. "Naah," he said. "I'd've heard something. I hear it all."

Later Nancy said the same thing to Kurt, "I think he's dead. Mr. Sanders' son. It's this feeling I have. It came over me."

We were sitting on the stoops in front of our rooms facing south. The moon was making a low, wide arc like a lantern being carried briefly across the night.

"Two years ago someone saw him," Alex said. "He wouldn't have just died, someone would have heard."

Nancy's voice was mournful: "I dunno."

Kurt stood. He put his arms up in the air, a gesture of surrender. "I feel like leaving the three of you here. You can walk home or wherever it is you're going." He left us, treading slowly to the car. We heard the door open and slam shut and then the motor starting, saw the flash of headlights as he pulled out.

"Did I say something?" Nancy asked. "Did I?"

Alex found it pretty funny, "Hey, do you think he really left us here?"

We sat for awhile thinking he'd probably come right back but he didn't. Alex got up and went to bed and so did I. I don't know how long I slept. It was a mosquito that woke me up. I tried to stop the noise by covering my head with a sheet, but it was too stuffy. I got up and felt my way through the dark to the door. When I opened it I saw Nancy was still sitting outside where I had left her. She must have heard me because she coughed a little and sighed.

"You waiting for Kurt?" I asked her.

"Kind of," she said. "What time is it?"

"I don't know."

"If he doesn't come back, how do we get out of here?"

"I don't know that either."

"He's *got* to come back. He left all his stuff in his room."

"What do you know about him anyway?"

"He's kind of weird." Then she laughed. "Sometimes I get the feeling everyone is weird. Don't you?" There was a noise just beyond us out in the grass, the sudden whisper of animals grazing in the night. A rush. A stop. Nancy stiffened. "What is it?" she said.

"Probably zebra." They were close, you could smell them, feel the heat they generated, but you couldn't see them, not until they were almost on top of you, patterns of black and white, so close you could reach out and touch them. I thought of Kurt the night before. I stood up and reached out. My hand hit a warm flank, a brush of stiff hair, wet and tense. In an instant they bolted.

"What did you do that for?" Nancy asked me.

"I don't know. I wanted to." I felt malevolent and I hoped Kurt *wouldn't* come back.

"Boy, you're just as bad as the rest of them. It must be catching," she said. "I mean I do not understand what you had to do that for."

Lights were coming on in the tents above us on the lawn in front of the lodge. The overlanders were beginning to shift and move around, getting ready to leave early, at dawn.

"We could go with them," I said. "They're going down to Dar es Salaam. That's where I was going anyway."

THE VISIT

In vain the stewardess warned everyone to be seated. There was to be an official inspection, she said. Behind Mrs. Dubois, a voice muttered, "Bloody hell." Then someone, a man, perhaps, wearing a gas mask, in a uniform that said Health Control, ran down the aisle spraying insecticide. Three large women who had boarded the plane in London wearing pantsuits, swooped out of the toilets, changed into caftans and curly wigs. On top of the wigs they had put loud, disturbing turbans starched into angles like enormous toy boats.

"Remain seated!" How the stewardess screamed at them, but nothing could hold them back. Men in billowing robes had risen and blocked the Health Control who had, it seemed, sprayed one of them, accidently or not, in the face.

"You don spray de *Oga!*" a voice was yelling, too shrill to have gender. At once they all grabbed the poor creature, tore off his mask and sprayed in revenge; his stricken face hung, strangulated and melting. The others were a mass of squinting eyes and opened, shouting mouths. Mrs. Dubois pressed a hanky against her nose and shut her eyes.

"Ladies! Gentlemen!" She could barely hear the stewardess, whose apron was dangling now. "Return to your seats."

"How bloody long must we wait on our arses this time?" It was the man behind Mrs. Dubois running out of patience.

Announcements came: "Photography in the airport environs is strictly forbidden," an unknown voice advised. For the stewardess was no more, or perhaps she was merely hidden behind a curtain. "Officials have the authority to confiscate all camera gear."

Landing cards were passed out: red for currency, pink for health, blue for immigration. There were instructions but these were muffled by the fight that was still going on around the Health Control. It had grown somehow as the plane filled with soldiers, which frightened Mrs. Dubois who had heard of coups and hi-jackings and seen enough pictures on television, until an officer, carrying a club and using it, called out, *"To your seats!"* He was as enormous as his voice so that she thought of Moses parting the waters. In the silence that followed, the stewardess appeared once more.

"Ladies and Gentlemen"—she seemed restored and had refreshed her lipstick—"the Nigerian authorities have granted us permission to deplane. Please file out in an orderly fashion."

Mrs. Dubois began looking for her daughter Beverly immediately despite the heat and darkness outside the plane. She experienced a slight dizziness common to moments of expectation like these when there can be no turning back. She grasped for the arm next to hers, offered or not, without even looking to see whose it was. Stairs to the asphalt below were endless; the arm stiffened as she clutched it. At the bottom, releasing her hold and looking up, she recognized the man who had sat behind her by his unkempt red hair which had begun to curl. His name was Harvey: a wife called to him.

"I'm just trying to help this nice colored lady," he answered, "before some rude bugger pushes her down."

Mrs. Dubois felt, by now, like the tiniest black speck on ankles nearly buckling beneath her. Finally she saw, beyond a wall of thick glass, pressed nearly flat by the thousands who jammed forward trying to see, her daughter Beverly waving a bright pink scarf. She waved back knowing that her hair had suffered terribly, when she wanted to look her best. She tried to smooth the frazzles into the neat bun she kept it in at the back. Even through the glass Beverly, too, looked exasperated but her hair was another story, done up in some astonishing fashion that was a thing unto itself, like a piece of furniture. Like a chair.

They hadn't seen each other for two whole years, and so it would not have been the right time to say, "Beverly Campbell, what *have* you done to your hair?" in the particular tones that Mrs. Dubois would have used. Or even to mention the way her daughter was dressed, in what looked like African clothes, a top of some kind with flounces that exposed too much, and a long skirt that appeared to be tied up, as if sewing machines had not been invented.

There was a flurry in which all the cards and Mrs. Dubois' passport were thrown about and stamped and her luggage opened and closed. All the while Beverly was urging her forward by wild gestures from the other side of the glass. It reminded Mrs. Dubois of a puppet show she had seen once. There was such a blare of voices and large heads in the way and these inflated men called Oga (a title, Mrs. Dubois suspected, that meant "sir" or "lordship," the only sign of manners she had seen yet) in their puffing robes and gold chains. And then, somehow, she was ejected into the crowd and Beverly hugged her and led her off in a series of quick motions.

"Where is Donald and the boy?" she finally asked when it was clear that her son-in-law and grandson had not come to meet her. There was only Beverly who was reaching for the luggage and shouting at the porters in a language that seemed to have English words in it but sounded foreign. She couldn't bring herself to say her own grandson's name, Adedayo. She had only seen it written but had never heard it and had a habit of changing it to David whenever she talked to friends or strangers. Now she was afraid that the name "David" would slip out, and Beverly would know everything.

"Oooooooo-ooo, Mama." Beverly said ominously, "Donald won't come to this airport for anyone except his *own* mother." Who was, in fact dead. Rather an irreverent joke, Mrs. Dubois thought when Beverly began to laugh.

They had to drive through the city of Lagos and to an island, Victoria Island, where, Beverly explained, most of the foreigners lived. They went in an air-conditioned limousine with a chauffeur, and because of the traffic, they went very, very slowly.

On the road, Mrs. Dubois saw how everyone was driving and knew she would never be able to describe it once she got home even if she could get pictures to prove it. Not like ordinary driving, but something else, although it was done in a car.

The only lights along the way came from little kerosene lanterns in front of wooden stalls where people, Beverly told her, were buying and selling things. There was a greenish cast to it all and sometimes red as they passed so slowly by, putting her in mind of terrible places where shadowy shapes swarmed on the edges to drag people down. A place like hell, Mrs. Dubois was thinking, though she wouldn't have said so to Beverly just then, so as not to hurt her daughter's feelings. Beverly's letters had been so excited, urging her to come for a visit, promising the greatest time. Even the palm trees which were associated with paradise looked ruined, barely survivors of war or hurricanes. Everything was either trampled down or heaped into great piles of trash, higher than the ramshackle houses and oily little sheds of the town.

Mrs. Dubois was thankful for the cool chariot and hoped the Lord could hear her. In her fingers, however, hidden underneath her purse and squeezed together, her arthritis began to act up and so the face she turned on those first images of Africa was one of pain.

Eventually they crossed a bridge and there were real houses with driveways and electricity as Beverly had promised. Street lamps and telephone poles emerged as proof of civilization.

"We live just a little ways down there," Beverly was saying. The road was empty now and pleasant as it passed a lot of new construction. Then it turned off into a circle of green lawns and driveways.

The Campbell's house was all lovely rectangles of light that rose behind glass over balconies. Beverly began by pointing out the lawn furniture. Then Donald, who trained accountants for Mobil Oil Company, appeared, naked to the waist, in what seemed to be a towel, as if he had just been caught in the shower. When he kissed his mother-in-law, she was aware of his chest as if she, too, had been stripped. Certainly she was engulfed by the flesh of his shoulders as they folded around her.

The baby, Adedayo—"We call him Ade," Beverly cooed, "which means crown,"—was being pressed excitedly into his grandmother's arms. Bare. And squirming. Were they *all* naked? It was as if she would never touch anything ever again but skin. The heavy perfume of a tropical flower, and the baby who had started to howl, overwhelmed her.

Inside, the house was full of what Beverly and Donald said was "African Art" and Mrs. Dubois did try to appreciate it. There were items, however, that she would have called hideous, certainly demonic, though Beverly assured her that it was all meant to scare away evil spirits. Or to represent natural phenomenon and, Beverly confided, female circumcision. About which Mrs. Dubois did not dare ask. All she said instead was, "But to keep them in a *home . . . ?*"

They had paused in front of a rotting bit of wood that might have been an ancient door post as Beverly claimed, though she doubted it. "To keep such things in your own home, where your child will see. . . ." She spoke too softly perhaps for Beverly or Donald to hear. In addition there were too many colors in the room and the clashing batik paintings which they had hanging in profusion.

Could this be her own Beverly June Dubois whom she had raised by her own hand in grace and simplicity? A widow, singlehanded, a nurse, in shoes and uniforms of white. Mrs. Dubois had always been certain that dignity took quiet, unassuming forms like elms or oak trees or pillars on porches, and had raised her only child in neat rooms where pastel colors dominated. Their small garden was cultivated with vegetables and flowers that had homely natures, like daisies—roses went too far, her father, an Episcopalian minister had maintained—and honeysuckle.

She was always tasteful in her dress and modest. Patent leather was the one concession she made to show although her hats ran to feathers but were otherwise moderate. She was nostalgic for the time when veils and gloves had been worn. It was a matter, she taught Beverly, of what you put on underneath that gave the outside layer its respectability. Long garments, slightly elastic, to hold the torso. Thighs kept in place by stockings even if they came in the wrong color and had to be dyed in coffee, a fragrance then fought with the right soaps or perfume. Now she was suspicious that Beverly had given up underwear entirely, for she had surveyed the laundry as it hung each day to dry. Climate, she wanted to tell her daughter, was no excuse. But it was as though her voice, worse yet, her very self was being silenced.

Her daughter seemed large and impossible, a span of exposed shoulders. The tops of her breasts were uncovered and there were usually beads around her neck, big hunks of things that looked like old beach rocks. In the forlorn humor of one who must submit, she wished she could think of some way to tell them that they were foolishly following nothing but their own pride and would suffer in the end, some clever way that would sound more like a joke. Just to make the point. No more.

As if on purpose, they served up meal after meal of what they referred to as "foo foo" in that appalling baby talk pidgin English that Donald found so entertaining. "Chop," which was supposed to be eaten with the fingers. She wouldn't, even if it tasted good, which it didn't. There was a contest every meal to see who could take in the most hot pepper. Dried things were what they ate, fish by the smell of them, blackened lumps that terrified her when she saw the cook poking at them in the kitchen. When she asked him what he was doing, he told her, "Cleaning de shit," a word he used with no particularity.

Mrs. Dubois could see herself getting thinner and thinner as her visit progressed, while they got fatter and fatter in testimony to their crimes against moderation.

One of their batik artist friends (who was famous in Europe, Donald said) took an evening meal with them, finishing off a small mountain of gooey, pounded yam and asking for more. His name was Aremu, a tall ugly man of vigorous bones and smiles. He had brought his latest "work," a wall-sized hanging, to sell. Unfurled and dangling in the living room, it seemed to alter everything, the world, the very universe, and made Mrs. Dubois choke. Beverly moved back and forth in front of it exclaiming. It was, the artist explained, a painting that had to be understood as myth. The creation myth, Donald clarified, nodding as if he had never heard of Genesis. Something about a chicken coming down from heaven and scratching around in the sand in a town called Ife, about a hundred miles away.

"But a chicken," Mrs. Dubois allowed, "is an ignoble creature." She was holding Adedayo, hoping Beverly would understand her.

There were many gods, Beverly was telling her, like Greek gods, which had been represented by Aremu—thunder, water, fire, all appearing as stalks on squat bodies. And something called "the female principle" that took the form of a woman's genitals grown into a creature with its own legs.

Mrs. Dubois heaved and let Adedayo drop in order to create a disturbance.

The smell of Donald's shaving lotion had become abusive; even her own perfume had taken a wrong turn. The humans in the dreadful batik were no more than triangles with breasts and arching penises. No abstraction could disguise it. Beverly was close to it now asking for more and more of the details, all of which Aremu was glad to supply. To make matters worse, a table of whiskey was rolled in like an altar and she knew they would go on all night.

"Beverly," she rehearsed, sitting alone in her air-conditioned room, "what is this *all* about?" Thinking of the time when Beverly had taken up with Donna Lassiter and was going around. "What is this that I hear, Beverly Dubois?" Because that was all it had taken in those days. But had she been right, in the end, to think that she was really the one who knew what Beverly wanted, even when she knew what was best? Was Donna Lassiter the early ripple of a current in her daughter's soul? Luxury. For a split second Mrs. Dubois felt shame instead of betrayal and noticed in the mirror that she had more gray hairs than a few hours ago. A chill of refrigerated air passed over her shoulder blades.

Perhaps it was only the place. Driving with Beverly to go shopping, she saw men on the sidewalks in pajama bottoms brushing their teeth or urinating into the open drainage ditches that festered everywhere, even in front of their own home on Victoria Island. Children squatted. Women came out and tossed tubs of garbage and soapsuds anyplace at all, even at each other. And they fought wearing lace brassieres as if they were normal clothes. None of this bothered Beverly who claimed she was "into it," and had developed a different laugh.

There was always traffic jammed up until it took over the sidewalks, and when they were stuck in it, vendors besieged them selling blouses that had breasts formed into them by bent hangers, or skin lightening creams which they tried to smear on their wrists. Once they were stuck for three hours and life settled in around them. Women set up stoves, cooked food and sold it. A girl in a nearby car gave birth.

Simple things were impossible. They had to stand in lines to get chits which told how much meat could be bought, or sugar, or beer, a form of rationing. A white or an obvious foreigner, or a rich Nigerian (made clear by his dress) was allowed to buy as much as he wanted, an unfair practice Mrs. Dubois accepted with a rigid spine and a frown even when the advantage was hers. These lines, she was sad to notice, turned Beverly aggressive, quite often rude.

"*Hey,* what is this?" Beverly had shouted once in a line where they got the chits to buy beer. "My mother is *American,* so you give her ten chits, not six." Though Mrs. Dubois did not drink beer at all.

The crowd, as usual, began to express its views. "Nabe guest-o," part of it contended. "Why you no give am de ten?"

The other part was shouting, "I say dis be our contry. Why we give de drink to foreign man?" in such a pent-up way she almost feared for her life.

"You *give!*" Beverly had put her head in the chit window and her hand almost in the clerk's face.

"Look am!" the clerk taunted; he had a flair. "Look wey dey don come from dis very Africa. No be de real Americans." He had a rumbling offensive laugh, however contagious it had become.

"Listen, you watch who you laugh at." Her own daughter Beverly had turned around and was shoving the person behind her. Mrs. Dubois dropped the six humiliating chits and stormed to the door. A huge man grinned down at her and winking, lifted her right off the ground and out of the way—diamond rings flashing and gold chains rattling and yards and yards of deep purple satin brocade. Behind him, although redundant, a skinny man was pushing shoppers out of the way and shouting, "Make de Oga go pass!" It was, Mrs. Dubois decided, a country of last straws.

"I am sure, Beverly," she said in the car, "that our ancestors came from some other part of Africa. A nicer part." It was the joke she had been looking for and Beverly was actually laughing. Sweetly, as though she saw the truth in it. For awhile they both laughed and the way home became easy. The traffic didn't seem so bad, and a wind had cleared away the overwhelming clouds so that the sky was reasonably appointed and the palms and philodendrons somewhat subdued.

There were times when she tried to broach the subject again without being certain what the subject was. "I never thought that Beverly would have been the kind to *shove* someone," she told Donald.

"Mama," Donald Campbell had answered, "this is no place to turn the other cheek," and laughed the whole issue into irrelevance. Beverly also saw humor in it and joined him as though they both were conspirators against the teachings of Christ. They were eating chips made of fried plantains which Mrs. Dubois found vaguely unpleasant. She could easily, at that moment, have blamed her son-in-law who was not the man he had appeared to be as little as two years ago. Beverly, however, confused her just as much.

On another occasion, she voiced her opinions of certain new acquisitions. "But Beverly, you used to like pretty things," referring to a collection of glass figurines that Mrs. Dubois still saved on the shelves in her daughter's old room.

Beverly began to talk about power symbols and images, rituals and the primitive vision. These, she claimed had been discoveries for her, a new way of seeing the world. But they were the crudest things and often in terrible condition like old chairs left on porches in the rain for years. Some of them had greasy rags attached to them or nails driven into them. One had a pouch in which there was (Beverly demonstrated) a shrunken bird. No, no, these were images which Mrs. Dubois needed to believe were obsolete, meant to be hidden in museums and looked at only by anthropologists who had perspective. Not kept alive in people's homes or in their minds. It looked, to her, too much like worship the objects were demanding.

"Who taught you about these things, Beverly?" She wanted to be exonerated.

"No one," Beverly answered.

"Certainly not I," the mother protested for she had learned only from her father and thought his was the way of life. In any case, it was sufficient.

"No, certainly not you, Mama," Beverly was saying. She had decided to pat her mother's head in a way that was close to insulting. It made Mrs. Dubois feel absurd and trapped. She would have struggled if she had known how, physically, to get away, but more than physical things were involved.

"Well, I hope you don't expect me to approve of this or even like any of it, any of it at all." She tried to extricate herself.

Beverly, on the other hand, had started to laugh. "Hey, you don't think we're pagans or something?" She was walking around in circles it was so funny.

"It wasn't that. You don't think . . . ." Everything blubbered out of Mrs. Dubois in little gasps. Perhaps they found her idiotic. "I can see there's no use talking," was all she could say finally, "about what I think."

Beverly looked a little wounded then and put on the pout she always used as a little girl to feign contrition. She seemed to be about to say something, as an apology or explanation, but chaos had erupted outside the house and the cook was running and shouting that little Master Ade had fallen in the drainage ditch and had emerged all covered in shit.

After that they began to bicker about little things, how much salt was appropriate and whether to cover the butter, which added tension to the simplest activities. Words were searched through to find hidden criticism. It caused Beverly to mope and Donald to be mildly sarcastic. It filled Mrs. Dubois with deep regret. She tried to be calm and stop making faces over the food and the batiks. She would endure; she told herself it was the most virtuous response, even as Beverly paraded out in more and more outrageous garments and flamboyant hairdos. Days had a biblical feel to them, of mothers and daughters in struggle, a thought that comforted Mrs. Dubois and drew her closer to the Lord. She thought of leaving Nigeria early, as a statement, but it looked too much like surrender and she sensed the danger in that. And so she stayed.

There was a beach on Victoria Island called Bar Beach. Often in the evenings, Mrs. Dubois and the Campbells, with Adedayo in a stroller, walked out past a small fishing village, to a woven shelter that Donald rented for pennies a month. They would sit under the shelter and watch the sunset while the baby dug in the sand.

The beach was open to the full force of the sea; you couldn't swim there or even wade without great risk. As many times as they went, on low or high tides, the water was never calm. Criminals were executed at one end of Bar Beach every Sunday afternoon in a garish atmosphere of vendors and celebration. Tied to posts and shot. Mrs. Dubois had seen pictures in the paper and sometimes, as it was getting dark and they were walking home, she felt a wave of nausea and attributed it to the terrible things that went on nearby. One of the most notorious, an infamous murderer called Baba-O, had been crucified and then shot. A blurred image on the front page of the *Daily News*, with its recollection of Christ, had horrified and insulted Mrs. Dubois who was only able to say, "Really, Beverly, what kind of people are these?" in a rhetorical fashion before going to her room.

Mrs. Dubois refused categorically to go near that end of the beach at all and made a big issue of it. They teased her all the time now, saying, "Oh Mama wouldn't like *that* . . . ," in a chorus which included Adedayo, while she ruffled and smoothed her clothes and looked misunderstood. It was a game by now in which the stakes were uncertain.

But they went to Bar Beach, to their own end of it, because, quite simply, they had to. It was a steep white slope of sand that rode into an ocean of changing colors. As the sun set, it grew red and the mist from the crashing waves was like pink and violet chiffon veils between them and the force of it. Sometimes there were pillars of light and the waves themselves, in perfect sequence, would rise like stairs to a marble temple. Sometimes the beach seemed to be set afloat and drifting far out. The clouds were angel forms then with great chains pulling them up over the churning water. It felt, Mrs. Dubois thought, like Zion, which she had never been able to imagine before.

One day, when Donald was working late, Beverly and Mrs. Dubois took the baby in the stroller and went to the beach. They passed the fishing village where men sat sewing nets of bright blue cord. Their huge black canoes were angled to the sea. When the tide was right, they would take the canoes into the surf, an amazing feat, bows held forward, high, arching in the crests to disappear and then appear again, only to face another wave, looming, crashing. Shining men held to the edges of the canoes. Mostly, however, the boats stayed quietly in line. From a distance they looked like so many reverends lifting prayer in unison. Until you saw the brightly painted symbols on the bows and down the sides. Beverly said these were of mysterious origin, possibly from ancient times. "Mesopotamia," she said, or perhaps long before that when black men first walked out from the center of Africa with all the secrets men would ever know, to find the oceans on either side. These were private theories, all her own, which seemed to grow in the presence of the magnificent canoes.

They strolled past women who were smoking hunks of fish over low fires or turning silvery minnows in the sun to dry. It occurred to Mrs. Dubois that these unsanitary activities had become familiar and less shocking. She didn't even wince when Beverly bought three cakes of fried dough, no more than brownish lumps, from a toothless old woman, to go with the iced tea they had brought with them in a thermos.

At the shelter they spread a small cloth and took out the tea and the lumpy cakes. It was still very hot and the sky, though blue, was tending to a yellow that it seemed to siphon from the green of the sea. Near the shore, the water was the palest green, like spring, deepening until it was almost forest black where it churned against the sky. She had to squint, and then saw patterns like visions in the pain and the brilliant shafts of light, as if her eyes themselves were wondrous and new.

"Well, I will surely miss this beach," Mrs. Dubois told her daughter. "This beautiful, beautiful beach!"

She had never, never in her whole life thought she would miss a beach. If it were frivolous, this feeling, she didn't care. She gave herself over to it in the same way the sky was surrendering to the sea.

"Yes, I certainly will," she repeated because it amazed her. "And even that village and the canoes."

It could have been wine she sipped instead of tea. She almost dozed, like Adedayo, whose head was there in her lap.

Then suddenly they were not alone. A group of people had come out from the village. Moving close together in a tight knot, there were at least twenty of them, men and women, moving and shifting as one across the sand. They were led by three men in long white robes and a two adolescent boys, also in white, who carried small wooden boxes. They were conspicuously silent. When they reached the water's edge, they spread apart and revealed a stretcher on which was the body of a child wrapped for burial.

"A funeral," Beverly whispered and assumed a better angle so she could see.

From the boxes, the young boys, who might have been acolytes of some kind, took candles and placed them in a row between the child and the water. Did the wind suddenly stop so they could light the candles that way? Or had there been a wind? Mrs. Dubois thought, on her life, there had been, but moments like this made everything uncertain.

A bowl was placed at the head and foot of the small figure. Then the women began to walk into the water and out again carrying water cupped in their hands to the bowls. The cloth wrappers they wore became wet and dragged in the sand, back and forth, back and forth, until the bowls were filled. Then they drenched themselves and shouted as the water poured from them. Their clothes hung like weeds. The men in the white robes began to speak lifting wooden staffs toward the sea. One of the acolytes beat a tambourine. They all began to wail as if calling out for help.

The tide, which had been coming in all the time, crept closer and closer to the body in the sand. Then, it was the queerest thing, the waves seemed to gather and lift the child in the air for a moment, as if he were in a cradle, and then they took the body, on the next swallow, gently, until there was nothing left but snuffed candles where the water had been.

Beverly shifted again and breathed, holding her mother's hand in attention. Rituals, she whispered to her mother, were open windows and she was peering in. It was all related to the business of power symbols or whatever Beverly went on about. Mrs. Dubois, on the other hand, had been swamped by an event that already had become something she would never dare speak of. And so she was silent, imprisoned by her daughter's clutching hand, until the party went, as it had come, quietly packed together. Was she the only one to have seen this thing?

Then it was over. Walking back, they remained silent, mourners for that dead child. The rest, the cradling wave, was something that absorbed her and she it. She could still see what had happened and the child's soul as it went softly into that thundering surf. In this way she journeyed farther than Beverly, without a private theory or even an answer.

At the house, Donald was waiting for them perched on a lawn chair. The artist, Aremu, was with him unrolling a new batch of batik paintings, their heads almost touching over the spreading cloths. Beverly, excited, rushed to see. Mrs. Dubois would always remember how they looked, illuminated, profile on profile on profile, as the cook, from inside the kitchen, switched on the garden lights.

Not much later, in America, in her own pastel rooms, Mrs. Dubois served tea to lady friends and talked about her trip to Africa. Parts of her story became most entertaining in retrospect—the Health Control, the way you did your shopping. Even an incident in which Beverly had to pull cash out from the brassiere of a market woman who was witholding change. Passing a dish of her famous gingersnap cookies, she told it all as one who had seen the humor in a riot and surprised her friends who had to fold their napkins before they dared to laugh. In the drainage ditch? Her own grandson? Covered with shit?

She especially liked to mention the Ogas without being able to say exactly what they were. They were emblems of a chaos that was too hard to describe. There was the crash of cups in saucers and the whispers of napkins opening again.

She had brought back a few things she thought were worthwhile if not beautiful, a fragile gourd with flower patterns etched carefully into it, an indigo-dyed cloth with bird designs painted on by chicken feather, a string of glass beads made in Venice and used in Africa for trading. Curiosities that anyone could appreciate.

Some of her friends were inspired and held the objects with a certain awe. She did not mention the art collection of Beverly and Donald and glossed over most of the questions about how they were. They lived in a very fine house, she would say, with servants and air conditioning, electricity and running water, because many of her friends had ideas about Africa that needed to be corrected.

"However," she would say in a suggestive tone, "though I am glad that I went, it's true, I'm not going to go back. You can believe that." And here she described the dried things people ate and the yams which, over there, were not at all the same thing as yams over here.

She kept the beach her own secret, the veils of mist, the pillars of light and stairs of mounting waves, except to say that there had been shocking executions: the vicious Baba-O who was crucified, like Jesus, and then shot while thousands watched. Against the crunch of gingersnaps and wringing napkins and the voices of her friends: "Oh my, oh dear, oh Lord."

MAKONDE CARVERS

Victory is a Makonde tribesman, a refugee from Mozambique and the Michaelangelo of Dar es Salaam. He dreams and carves in ebony in a ramshackle shed on the main road out of town. He's an old man, known to be the best. Victory gets the biggest logs. He takes the snarled and twisted bases, flips them so the hard black fingers of root leap into the air or flattens them on one side and drops them to the horizontal to find his shapes and pictures. Sometimes he leaves the cortex of white wood, cuts in toward the ebony like a peeping Tom. He only sculpts *shetanis,* the devil spirits that haunt the forests and tidal waters of the East African Coast. The carver is as gnarled and black as his blocks of wood. He waves me in from the road to see what he's just finished.

Victory has two new carvings, a small one displayed high on a pedestal of uncarved trunk, a big one still on the ground. Oh yes, old Victory, I'm thinking, I can see you've winked together these demons with a laugh. I can see your tongue in your cheek. These must be two of the wildest things you've ever done.

He fingers the big one, cut from a mighty and twisted stump. On its thick lump of body the devil has about five legs bent at the knees, feet pressed out where the roots once grew. A human head rests on one set of knees. Behind it there's a demon's head with pointed ears and many eyes. Arms are everywhere. Miscellaneous. Nondescript. Something like a tail, more likely a penis, drops out of one set of loins, winds around and somehow ends up in the demon's mouth.

"He's swallowing himself," Victory explains. "It's a man-eating *shetani* that hides in anthills. When a man comes to the anthill to get dirt for his bricks, the *shetani* gobbles him. But not in this case because the *shetani* has been visiting this very man's wife, so something comes out which is causing him to swallow himself." A typical *shetani* story: humans and their demons, their endless tangles. The other log is carved on its side. It has lion's legs, a dog's head and the body of a fish. Along the back fin are many small heads which Victory explains start screaming whenever fishermen piss in the sea.

I tell Victory, teasing, "No one will buy these!"

"They will buy," he insists.

Of course, he's right: he knows the trade well. Once, searching for the vision behind this art, I asked him if the *shetanis* represented his private mythology.

He laughed at me. "Foreigners love them," he answered.

Victory is the most popular carver on the road. European tourists hear of Victory before they come on safari. And he's a skilled con man. He has somehow convinced me to buy too many of his *shetanis.* I don't have any idea how I will get them home. They're all in the corner of my tiny living room, a forest of ebony carved to madness. I have a *shetani* who gives birth from its head like Hera. A *shetani* with a womb like a porch where babies grow like potted plants. A *shetani* who has intercourse with trees and grows leaves for hair. A modern times *shetani* that dwells in piles of old tires: its head is a lightbulb, its ear a radio receiver and it has a telephone in its gaping mouth. I have the dread chameleon *shetani* that prowls the night and when, in a dream, a human soul comes out to peek around, it flicks its long coiled tongue like a flame and catches it forever.

Victory tries to get me to commission him for his next piece. He says he knows someone who has an old and enormous log, a venerable block, from a time, more than fifteen years ago, when there were still some big trees left. Victory needs a lot of money to buy the ebony. Even if he sells these two new pieces, he won't have enough money for it.

What he wants to carve on the big log is a *shetani* story of the Fall. It seems that when the serpent gazed in hatred on the Garden of Eden, two *shetanis,* the Adam and Eve *shetanis,* were born in the jealous reflection of his eyes. They resembled the humans so closely that it was impossible to tell which was which. They had human brains but inside they were made of fruits. Instead of hearts they had mangoes. Instead of stomachs they had breadfruits. Instead of livers they had guavas. Eve's breasts were oranges, Adam's penis a banana. They were expelled from Eden with the other two, but still wander around the world undetected. At night they open and their fruits fall to the ground where the seeds germinate and trees and plants spring up and produce fruits. If humans eat these, they are stricken with envy. Only witch doctors who have looked on the Adam and Eve *shetanis* can recognize these hellish trees. There's a tree, Victory points out, there near his shed which bears such poisoned mangoes. The old man grins as he talks: his teeth are filed to points.

On this one mighty trunk, Victory plans to tell the whole story. The tall back portion will be an afflicted tree, near it a human tortured by jealousy. In front and below will stand the Adam and Eve *shetanis* as they appear by day and in back and below as they are at night, opened, dropping their evil fruits.

One day Victory's shed is abandoned. I stop to see his brother Musa who has a shed on the same road closer to town. Unlike Victory, Musa doesn't work alone: he's got a factory of some ten or twelve carvers chipping away under the wide umbrella of an old mango tree. Six of them are hunkered around an elephant's tusk, a real prize, four curving feet of ivory. They're arguing about who will have what portion of the thing. One of Musa's carvers is already offering to sell me ivory bangles on commission if I will bring him American things on trade—Timex watches, levis, razor blades, Jack Daniel's.

Musa asks me if I can get him some batteries for his radio-cassette player. There are no batteries left in the country, he tells me. He believes that Americans have shipments and commissaries, can get anything anywhere at anytime for prices lower than any African could ever dream of. Musa's face is elaborately etched with scars and tattoos. Something like cat's whiskers radiate from his nose and up his cheeks. Between the whiskers are jagged lines like lightning. His forehead is striated with verticals.

Musa's usual request is for me to arrange a marriage between him and an American girl. It's a big joke, but he presses me with such enthusiasm that I almost believe it's possible. Our routine: he's willing to pay two tusks as a bride price. I tell him he'll have to build her a flush toilet and buy her a car: he says can do, if I promise him one with very long and shining hair—black hair or tea-colored hair, he is not interested in any blonde hair the color of dead grass. He laughs. There's a triangle chipped between his two front teeth.

Musa's story today is that the government is moving to take the ebony away from the carvers, declaring that all the trees now belong to them. Only the government will be able to cut and sell the wood. Two years ago it was the same with ivory. Now the Makonde have to buy all their ivory from poachers and pay heavy bribes to cover their tracks. They don't make any profit on ivory anymore, but keep it in their sheds as a come-on: it's what the tourists want. If the government takes the trees, the Makonde will lose all their profits, all their motivation. Musa says they'll go back to Mozambique then and do their business in cashew nuts.

There's a rumor that the government is getting ready to send the army into the Makonde villages to seize their logs and force the carvers to buy the wood back at a controlled price. "We will have to close our sheds," he tells me. Victory, he says, has closed for good. But Victory, Musa adds, has been commissioned by a certain French woman who paid him a very big advance on a very big trunk which he has taken to the bush to carve in secret. When it is finished the French woman has promised to pay him a very, very, big price. The Fall.

I meet this French patron of the arts at Musa's shed a few weeks later. She's buying ivory bangles. Her name is Virginie. Her husband works at the French Embassy. Miraculously, for someone who lives in the tropics, she has avoided a sun tan. She's as white as porcelain, yet she doesn't seem pale, rather glazed and tinted like an antique doll. The ivory is barely visible on her fine wrist. She has very dense, very blonde, straight hair clipped into a neat page-boy. And she's plumed: the pastel sundress has a tiered skirt, a floral print.

We share our interest and enthusiasm for Victory's work. She says she owns six of his *shetanis.* "Everything else is rubbish," she says.

"He is so wonderful, so *ingénu.*" She watches me, tips her head looking for some English.

"I would have said he's savvy," I tell her.

She knows the word, forgives the sin on her language, and smiles. "*Mais non, non,*" she says. "He is *naturel, ingénu,* there is no question."

I ask another question. Perhaps he does not know he is an artist? If he does not know, then is it art he makes—or totem?

"You have to ask this about all primitive work, *non?* But he is not primitive." She shook her head. "It is a problem."

"He's an old phony," I answer.

But she's serious. "You see, I wish to write on this question in a book. A book on the subject of African Art. I have no training," she sighs. "But I do not think training is so important."

She has a bright clear smile as beautiful as a child's. Her elegant fingers come to rest on her collar bone, nails painted white, heavy gold rings.

"I have made so many notes here and in West Africa." She looks at the ground, then works her fingers into that heavy hair.

"For too long I have been a model. An *objet.* I tire of it. I wish to do something different now."

She looks up but her eyes miss mine, embarrassed, and wander out from the shed to what must be her car, a black

Mercedes Benz with diplomatic plates, a French flag in the window.

"I am going to see Victory now," she says. "Perhaps you like to come, *non?*"

"Yes, I'd *love* to come," I tell her. "So you have really commissioned the Fall."

She nods, waves Musa toward the car. "Musa will show us where he is, of course," she says. "But please, you must not say it is phony!" She hurries, smiling, opening car doors for us.

The Merc has air conditioning and leather seats. In the few minutes it takes to seal us off from Africa, the heavy smell of the leather fades and Virginie's perfume comes to life—crisp and light, roses from another hemisphere. There's no sound. The Merc's engine is tuned to silence and we float along on its fine suspension with no thought of the rough road. Sealed off, we watch the tropics screened there on the tinted windows of the big car.

According to Musa, the sculptor is working in a compound hidden in the cashew plantations that stretch along the coast north of the town. Makonde farmed cashew in Mozambique and they feel at home among the low, lush trees. They brew a traditional wine from fruits after the nut has been removed. "The government owns the trees and the nuts, but we can take the fruits," Musa says. "For beer." He grins.

Virginie drives the Mercedes into the plantation as far as it can go. We open its doors and our icy space is blasted, the chill conquered in an instant. There's a smell of ripening, fermenting cashew fruits as though someone has been washing everything in cheap perfume. Musa leads the way up a steep rocky path. Virginie's spike sandals creak and bend like stilts, but she, expertly and gracefully poised on them, hops like a ballerina to the top.

Victory is holed up in an enclosure of nine or ten thatched mud houses. Most of the Makonde men are away in their sheds, chipping ebony, carving ivory, smoking *bhangi,* and listening to their radio-cassette players. Makonde kids by the hundred are running around chewing on sugarcane. Young Makonde women are pounding things in big mortars while old Makonde women sit in the redolent cashew shade smoking pipes and cigarettes. Most of the old women have lip plugs, small flat disks implanted below their noses in their upper lips. One story has it the Makonde put these plugs in to keep the Arab slavers away from their women. Then they got to like it. The sight of Virginie in the compound, like a butterfly, fluttering and landing in their midst balanced on those high pedestals turns every head in the place.

Out back, half in the reeking yellow shadows of cashew trees and half in the sun, old Victory is finding the source of man's biggest problem in an ebony log. He's finished carving out a stumpy looking tree, trunk as thick as the crown, leaves cut in raised relief, veins and stems etched lightly into the wood. On the top, like a bromeliad, in a basket of slender, arching fronds, a pineapple of all things, the envy-soaked *shetani* fruit which the old genius has somehow made to look juicy, ripe and delicious.

"But it is *marvelous!*" this Virginie says. She sways on those needle heels and her dress hums like cicada wings.

Victory is all grins. He immediately raises the price, like

a spoiled film director going over the budget, and she, like some eager Hollywood backer, without hesitation, agrees to pay.

The government not only claims ownership of all the ebony but it begins to close the sheds declaring all private enterprise against the law. Along the road nothing is left of the sheds but bare patches of ground, the haphazard remains of old roofing—stretched burlap, cardboard, thatch, corrugated sheetmetal. I stand with Musa in the ruin, in the white ivory sawdust and black ebony wood chips. There are no wisps of hash in the air, no high-life cassettes jumping in the background, no rhythmic tapping of the chisels and the knives on the wood.

Musa is not dressed for work today. He's wearing a pair of designer bell bottom blue and white striped trousers, red plastic platform shoes, a fluorescent orange T-shirt, a pinstripe wool vest and a white linen sports jacket. He wonders if he would have any luck migrating to America and opening a business selling carvings. "Americans like these," he says. "I could get lots of customers." I imagine Musa's shed on the Jersey Turnpike, and the sign:

WELCOME TO M-
AKONDE CARV-
ERS NATIVE
ORIGINEL ART

The big problem is getting his money out of the country. The Tanzanian currency doesn't convert. His only choice is to buy goods here and carry them back to Mozambique. Trouble is there are no goods. He's afraid that when he crosses the border to home, he'll be flat broke.

Not long after the last shed closes, I meet Virginie in Patel's Department Store waiting in line to buy butter. She has the following story: Victory was recently caught by the army with a lot of illegal ebony. They seized it all including the piece he was working on—the Fall, nearly completed. The old man was released but some official decided the work was a national treasure. "Even though," she says, "he is not a national." They sent it to the museum where it was labeled an antiquity so no one could remove it from the country. They have put it, Virginie claims, in an ignominious display case where it will die along with the whole continent. Since the French are so terribly unpopular here, her embassy connections have been no help at all in her claim on the carving. She has been to see it several times in the museum.

"It's absolutely marvellous," she sighs. "Ah it's a pity *we* have lost it. I have not even made a photo of it. For my *great* book." She eyes me ironically. "Everyone says, 'No, Virginie, she will never do this book.'"

Today she's wrapped in soft blue cotton, her lean body like a dragonfly's just visible beneath its wings. She is flushed with disappointment: there seems to be no hope of her getting the carving. She and her husband will return to Paris in a few weeks and Victory, she says, has gone back to Mozambique with his brother Musa. She speculates that very soon all the carvers will be gone. Rumors are that the government wants to nationalize *them,* take them to some big warehouse near the airport where they can sit and carve their statues but not sell them. The government will pay them the same wage they pay everyone else.

Virginie and I go around to the museum then to have a final look at the Fall. They've put it in the back of a dusty case with a few other Makonde artifacts—totem dolls, cap masks, and yellowing photographs of facial decorations from an old exhibit.

"There, you can see for yourself," Virginie says. Perturbed, her toes wiggle in the confines of her lacy sandals, nails painted a shimmering opalescent white. "This really is his very best," she mopes.

It probably is. The old bugger has got it all on there, even two tiny desperate figures carved midway up the devil tree—the real Adam and Eve. Of course, everyone in the carving is a Makonde. Eve has a lip plug and Adam looks oddly like Musa. The serpent coils at the base of the carving, huge, with Makonde facial designs along its body. The *shetanis* seem to have just popped from its eyes. Theirs are marked by inlaid red glass beads. These two devils do not seem ashamed at all about the recent events in the Garden: they haven't put on any fig leaves and seem ready to go out and make trouble without a second thought. The back of the carving is against the wall where we can't see it—the unzipped Adam and Eve *shetanis* driven from Paradise like netherworld johnny appleseeds up to no-good. Above it all the awful fruit looms. It's too bad Paris will miss this piece. I have a feeling standing in the shabby museum that it's all too bad, that Virginie's burning questions about art and about herself will have to go unanswered, and that I am going to miss Victory and the sheds.

But Virginie is wrong and so am I. The white races have a history of being wrong about Africa. All the Makonde don't leave Dar es Salaam. Victory doesn't leave. Less than two months later a few sheds start to open again. I'm sure it's illegal and that they're all paying bribes and banking on government inefficiency. Maybe they figure the government has forgotten them. Maybe it has.

Victory opens in the remains of Musa's shed and a few of the old carvers are back on the job, chiseling away on their logs and their tusks and conning tourists. One of the young carvers, high as a kite, is waving strands of ivory beads at a bunch of Italians from the embassy who have come with a carload of goods for trade—mostly old clothes. Victory has got another bunch of Italians standing around him as he works on a long twisting piece of ebony which bursts with many shapes.

He tells them what it is—the termite *shetani.* It flies at night after a rain and steals the dreams of humans who make the mistake of opening their eyes before the dream has gone. These dreams are deposited in a piece of wood where they hatch into larva. The larval dreams eat at the wood reshaping themselves to haunt the humans from whom they were stolen. The piece shows the darkling termite, huge wings folded at its side, big ant eyes, facets breaking the ebony, like obsidian, into sharp edges and shining planes. From its abdomen drops a string of screaming and laughing human heads and from the log below their dreams erupt.

Victory has only finished two, a tiny man with a huge erection, floating in a cushion of breasts, a tiny woman perched in a flower, her hair becoming petals. What other dreams was this man about to eat into that wood? *Ingénu?* At least one of Virginie's questions has been put to rest by this piece. His laugh at all of it—his serious jest. But what if Virginie had been robbed by that flying fiend in the night—her dream, the one she opened her eyes on too soon, the unfinished one, what image would its larva have raised in the carver's log?

"You're the termite *shetani,*" I tell him. My hand is on that squirming wood. "How much do you want for it?"

He grins. His price is enormous, but I know if I bargain long and hard enough, he'll con me into buying it.

MY MERMAID

When we first met, Corinne was dressed in pale blue. She wore her thin red hair like her daughter's, in bangs and loose to her collar, nervously brushing it or holding it back with her fingers. We barely noticed Sid, her husband, and could not have recognized him the next day had they not been together. They had come to Ethiopia, she announced like an M.C., from a small campus in Colorado where he had been the head of the music department ("the youngest ever!"). His instrument was the voice but his great love was ethnic music. He was an authority. Had written *a book.* Yes, she said, it was the thrilling sounds from *here* that had made them drop everything and come running. As Peace Corps volunteers. As anything. Any way they could.

From the beginning Corinne thought we were friends, but I never really liked her much. I did feel, however, somehow inclined toward her. Perhaps I was only curious. Perhaps it was because she seemed to think she had some special affinity with me, I can't imagine why. She was, I suspected, fashioning her drama on the spot, taking a part in it that she knew was better suited for someone else. It was diverting at first. I was her audience, providing simulated applause, wondering if she would let me backstage. One morning I really thought she had stepped out of her disguise. She needed someone to talk to and had called on me.

"I'll tell you everything," she had breathed toward me the evening before. We had met unexpectedly on the street. "I'll call you tomorrow and we can meet someplace to talk."

I really thought she wouldn't call but she did and we met "that morning."

"Sid's left me." I knew. The word was out. "It's been coming—" she whispered coyly, "oh, you could never believe how long!" She had never been happy with Sid since the first year of their marriage. When they married, she said, they had "harmonized." But over the years she had become his shade, no more. And true, when we first met, she had rattled on loudly about his brilliance and success as if his achievements might cast a flattering light on her, might make her visible. That morning she told me that everything he had accomplished had been drained from her. Each success of his had withered her talent, her ambition. He had closed her in, buried her alive.

"It was calculated, too," she swore, "the kids, the house in the woods miles away. No friends. I mean a real trap. I only noticed it when I was nearly done in." In a burst of strength she had prepared to leave him, ". . . and then this job in Ethiopia appeared. It seemed a chance. So he agreed to take it as an offering to me. *To me!* 'Oh, we'll do everything you want this time,' he said, 'I'll change.' Well, as you can see, he didn't change. Of course, *I* have."

"You know," she went on, "at first I thought he might just do it. And Ethiopia is so fantastic. It was like coming alive, and when I woke up from that long sleep, the first person I saw was Sid—like Adam and Eve." She had her hand in her hair; her eyes spiraled. "Like Adam and Eve before the Fall," she laughed.

"Only he couldn't take it," and she went on and on about her plans; a job, research, travel. "I'm going to do some composing again," she throbbed, ". . . all new, a musical imagery I never dreamed of before." For the moment I believed her. You could almost say, I believed in her.

When we first met, we had seen them often. A Peace Corps training program threw us together. The other trainees spoke of Corinne and Sid as "hard to take." Everyone thought they were nuts. For openers, they had come, flagrantly ignoring Peace Corps regulations, with their pets, a huge German shepherd and an ancient Siamese cat. They refused to join the group in the small flats rented for Peace Corps families during the training period and decided, rather loudly, to stay on at the Menen, a relic of a hotel the Italians had built ages ago in what had become a reeking crime-ridden corner of the city. The rest of us opted for the flats. Ours was seven stories over the city. Corinne came once to see me there. I took her to my balcony into a sky as sharp as ice.

"Yes, it's very nice," she sighed, "but not for us. No, we'll stay at the hotel!" It was then that she told me about her wonderful marriage where interests were shared yet individuals and talents respected. "It isn't a question of compromise," she told me, "compromise only gives you a part. It's a matter of affirmation, of having the space to grow and the confidence to will. The hotel life will give us room. It will put us in touch. The girls will learn. And Sid and I . . ." She had it all worked out.

Later I told my husband, Roger, "Corinne Davies says that they are staying at the Menen for—hold on!—not just the training program, but for the whole two years!"

"She's going to walk down the hall to the toilet for two years?" he asked, laughing.

"So she says. Listen," I went on, "they have this idea about a new life style. Breaking away. They want to confront something. Ethiopia, or something."

"That hotel has nothing to do with Ethiopia," he said.

"But she has a plan in mind; maybe they cooked it up together. They want a change.

"I think," I went on, "they have this idea that the Menen is some kind of commune!"

"They won't stay there. There's no way."

"You know what kills me," I said, "is her straining to be so eccentric. I don't know—different, better. Happier! She wants me to admire her. To envy her."

At that point we saw them nearly every day. We had language classes together. During the breaks between classes we would seek the sun. The classrooms of the old stone building were cold with the heavy rain. If we were lucky the clouds would break and the sharp highland sun would blaze into the courtyard. Corinne and I would lean together on a wall. She'd tell me how well the hotel was working out. Life surged and played. The language had come alive. Saturday night parties—drums and flutes and lyres. She was like some kid back at school in September fighting for the honor of having had the best summer. And she wore the clothes of a little girl—full skirts, pastels, pretty flats and those bangs.

Sid was the opposite. Almost dull. Very serious. She claimed he studied Amharic every night, but he was too shy to try and speak the language so he never seemed to improve. He was "intense," she said. He was that kind of man. They went about as lovers, arm in arm or holding hands. She was always gazing up at him or fretting over him like a girl friend. One day I followed them on the street. She darted birdlike in and out of small shops, her movements fast and jerked. He was angled back, his shoulders almost prideful. Was he so different when they were alone? She turned suddenly as though she felt my stare and passed her eyes over me with a nod, a smile, and not a word.

As the training program progressed, Sid and Corinne drew close to the college students who were our language teachers. Kassahun Abate became their special friend, and they at last requested that he become their teacher exclusively, give them a private class. He was the best, she told me; they wanted him alone. They became almost inseparable. They went everyplace together. He was good to their girls and helped them carry their things. They shared private jokes.

Like many Ethiopians, Kassahun was overwhelmingly handsome; his large almond eyes were dark with intelligence. Corinne, I noticed, flirted with him in her darting, almost silly, way. She sought him with her eyes and touched him whenever she could. She told me every chance she had what a superior person he was. She felt some destiny had brought them to Ethiopia. Something more than coincidence. Didn't I see it? How she and Sid and the girls had truly become Ethiopians themselves. I wondered if Sid fancied himself an Ethiopian. He looked like someone who was just tagging along. In the shadows of her delight and renewal, the man was fading.

On weekends our group was often taken outside the city on day trips. Sid carried a store of camera gear—lenses, meters, tripods. Corinne brought a cassette recorder. They were after, she explained, first impressions, how they saw the country before time and familiarity had colored their views. She always insisted on sing-alongs but had to coax Sid to get him to lead. His voice was strong and beautiful, but his eyes, so distant from that voice, were always annoyed.

One Sunday we went to a hot springs where the Italians had carved out a beautiful garden and a large pool. Sid didn't swim; he never even took off his shirt. He wandered around with his camera seeking an eagle that had darted over us and veered toward a nearby tree. She was a good swimmer, bounding, playing and dancing as if she had been born for the day. She lay stretched in the sun, her pink skin turning very red.

It was a splendid day; the sun glazed. I drifted in the warm water listening to the drone of a nearby radio. Little things about the past few weeks floated into place; I pulled them through the water, dissolving, seeking only my breath in the rhythm of each stroke. Nothing much existed but the hissing of the air through my teeth into my lungs. Nothing much, I should say, but the woman whom my eyes caught skimming the water so close to me. Why did she loom so large? Like those great pink Picassos that run along the beach, she filled my eyes. I felt instinctively that she couldn't go on with it much longer.

The day laid its patterns on the pool, on the lawns. The eagle's shadow. Sid alone, pale, curved against a tree, bent over his camera. Corinne cut out against the green water. Kassahun at the pool's edge, his wide sun hat a frame for his magnificent face. We separated into small groups and shifted on lawns woven with shade. We played games. It went along without a sound.

Until we left. Packed into the bus that brought us, her voice shattered the clean quiet of the afternoon. She laughed and talked, changing seats like her daughters who couldn't settle. She visited her way pushing down the center to where the boys sat. Kassahun Abate put his large straw hat on her head. I watched. Did I stare? Was I obvious? They sang, her soprano loud and professional over all the rest.

Alemé, one of our teachers, sat beside me, her head bent toward the singing. "An Ethiopian man," she said after awhile, "would simply beat his wife. And the other women," she laughed, "would say, 'That one is uncircumcised.'"

But he couldn't beat her. Sid wasn't an Ethiopian man for all her desire to make him one and as I watched him there alone, I fancied his sad expression came from an idea he had that she should be someone else, someone with a gentle music to draw him on. His youngest girl was asleep on his lap, and his eyes, fixed above the child and focused straight ahead, were blank. If he had spoken then, would he have told of disappointment? Was this what was on his face? His silences as I read them at that moment were mystery bound in dream. It made her song no more than bellowing; loud but shallow.

In time it was clear that she was winding the spring of their tensions as tight as she could.

"You know," she said one day as we talked of our lessons, "Kassahun always shows us how subtly a word can change. Like," she grinned, *"memTat."*

"MemTat?" I asked. "It means to come."

"Uh-huh. But if you say *memtat* with the soft *t* it means 'to beat'. He said it to me one day. *Emetalehu*. Like a whip. I will come. I will beat. And the air," she breathed, her face flaring, "crackled with sex."

I drew the picture for Roger. "Of course!" he said, "How did we miss it?" Perhaps it was the fifteen years that separated them. Or the culture. Perhaps it was her constant fawning over Sid. Perhaps it was the racial thing.

"She couldn't resist telling me, you know," I said, "She had to give it away. I'd been watching and I think she knew. She felt me looking at her."

The shape made a triangle now. Age-old. We were sure Sid knew. I mean, if the air was crackling with sex, Sid surely felt it. But nothing happened right away.

As our training program drifted to a close, we saw less of them. If I ran into her on the street, she'd tell me how wonderful everything was. Sid's job at the university was great. She couldn't say enough about Kassahun Abate who had become, she claimed, like a son. Already they had promised to take him to the States when they returned.

Giddy with pictures of them, I fashioned a drama set at the Menen against a background of crumbling walls and dark wood, smells of roasting coffee and garlic frying: Pushed by Sid, she had faced her feelings, the desire for Kassahun. There had been scenes. Yes, a Pirandello script of innuendo because the children were always there. Sid called her selfishness to task; issued ultimatums. She told him that she had not slept with Kassahun. In this way there remained a purity she saw a danger in risking. Their lust alone was all she wanted and needed.

"Don't be so dumb!" Roger roared. "She is, too, sleeping with him!"

"Can't be. Sid wouldn't just take it."

"He loves it. It means he doesn't have to sleep with her."

I laughed but went on, parodying Corinne. "Still, she is sticking firm to Sid and the work. They're going to lift it to the level of their hopes!"

Roger, the audience, clapped. " 'The level of their hopes'? I say they're doing something else."

"What else?"

"She's fucking Kassahun for one thing."

I snickered. "Have you seen them?"

Of course, we had seen very little of them.

From the Menen they had moved into a large villa together with about twenty musicians. They were, we guessed, going to turn it into a real commune. "Sid's idea(!)," Corinne informed me, was to create an orchestra from the group to perform the music he collected. They would *live* the music. The house would *be* music.

I went to visit to see this. The house was like a Tuscan villa. The walls were earthy golds, polished red tiles were on the floor. "Our house in the States was contemporary," she told me, "but this—ah! It's just what the girls want. Old-fashioned. Worn and lovely." She ushered me around. "This is our room," she said, "and this is for Kassahun." She looked as though she were in another world.

"Kassahun? Is he in this orchestra of Sid's?"

"Uh-huh. The business manager. Our field trip guide."

"And the university?"

"He quit. He'll go in America when we go back," she paused, making a strange humming sound, "if we go back."

The house was full of people. It had made the dog nervous and he paced on the verandas or whined in the corners. The old cat basked in the sun.

These days Corinne had taken to wearing Ethiopian dress which made her look even more like a child—the white gauze cloth with embroidered borders, the gathered skirt, the soft shawl over her shoulders. Gaily she sat me down to a cup of tea and took out pictures of their house in Colorado. She was smiling in most of them. There on a cantilevered balcony with mountains behind her. There by the tall narrow windows of the house, the sharp lines framing her body.

"Like the house?" she asked.

"Nice," I said absently.

"Everything was, you know—contemporary. Bright rugs. The couch was lemon yellow." She shook her head as if she hardly recognized it. "The dining room was chrome and leather. That," she stopped, "is what we gave up. People work a lifetime for it. But we saw that we were giving up the world. You know what I mean, I think? It wasn't enough. We wanted something great."

I didn't see her much after that, but when I did, she added to the list of her joys. She and Sid (and Kassahun!) had travelled around, collected music. They were making discoveries. It was what she had dreamed of and it was happening. She often begged me to visit, but the few times I went there, they were out.

The house bristled with a growing population. One day I caught her on the street. "How's it going?" I asked.

"Oh," she waxed, "I wonder how we ever lived so long alone!" She made me promise to come on the holiday for sure. "Bring Roger," she urged.

So I dragged Roger there on the morning of Meskel, the feast of the True Cross, the end of the long rains. She bounded down the steps of the villa. It was her style, all delight, a nervousness of flowers pinned in her hair, dancing down the stairs wearing a flowered dress scooped at the neck and matching the dresses of her daughters, only now, because she was losing weight, a bit too big, her bra fully visible in the V of her back. She came down carrying a host of yellow Meskel flowers, smiling over them at us. Would we stay for tea? And there was Sid lost in the slow sloping of his shoulders, alone in the room too big for their furniture. He seemed impatient with the disorder of the children and aloof from the hurly-burly of the house.

Then before the tea was served, she hurried in to say that she was going off with Kassahun and leaving us to tea with Sid. Alone with Sid! We exchanged glances. What would have happened if we had asked him then? As it was, his eyes gave absolutely nothing away, his face was impenetrable. The moment was awkward—that tray, the extra cup. He seemed to want us gone and we would have left. But after all, we had to stay.

He was sorting his slides with a small hand viewer and he offered them to us shyly, the record of his first few months. I must confess I expected more from the pictures. They were flat and uninteresting, telling nothing of him and very little about the country. But there was one remarkable picture—his wife at the hot springs. She was sitting on a rock, in the distance, dwarfed against the green water of the pool. She appeared there, slender in the waist, a tiny silhouette in a shimmer of sun, and his title, "My Mermaid" was written out in black marker across the frame. It shocked me, not because his image of her was so out of whack with what she seemed to me, but because I had suspected it already. And I was surprised that so secret a man as he had written it out and handed it to me, ignoring the embarrassment of the tea, her cup untouched, the house gone suddenly silent (was it silent or had I just stopped hearing?) the moment dry and smelling of doom. Three weeks later he was gone.

Roger knew it first. "Sid left this morning!"

"Sid left?" I said, "And Corinne?"

"She wants to stay. She refused to leave. Rita Black said Sid was totally out of control. 'Sobbing,' she said, 'unable to stop. No Corinne in sight.'"

"Sid left," I breathed, softly, as though I hadn't expected it.

"Do you suppose," I said, "that he actually *didn't* know about Kassahun? That he only just found out?"

"He knew," Roger answered. "Something else broke him."

Now, "that morning," she seemed so straight, so right. I had no choice but to believe her. She seemed different. She seemed to have matured in the short time since Sid had left. She came to me with her hair tied back in a scarf, the bangs gone. She wore white slacks and a silk tailored shirt. She had lost more weight and the slenderness was becoming. The angles of her face appeared and she moved with grace, the bounce gone. She had slowed down, her anxiety fading with his departure. I could only believe her, though as she walked away under the fierce light of that highland sun, into the distance she appeared slight and ghostlike, fairly vanishing from my sight.

How long she lasted after that I'm not sure. I heard that she left the villa and moved to a small house with Kassahun and the girls. Rumors flew. No one had seen them. The girls were no longer at school. And then one day we heard that she had been taken away. "Under sedation," said Rita Black. A doctor had accompanied her to the States. Rita said something about how Sid had tied up their money and forced her back. Starved her out, so to speak. The Ethiopian government would not give her a work permit and Kassahun clearly had nothing.

"So he won!" shouted Roger in an I-told-you-so voice. "I really couldn't imagine that he would leave his kids over here. She was bonkers. What she told you 'that morning' was her biggest lie. You know," he said, "it may have been the other way around all along."

"The other way around?"

"Sure. She was dependent on *him,* trying to intrude on *his* talent, trying to suck *him* dry. When she had him nearly finished (where she wanted him) she threw Kassahun at him. She may have been left isolated in Colorado because no one could stand *her.*"

"All beside the point," I said. "He was developing his music and she was losing hers. She was terrified. That, my dear, is what it really is about."

"So she made him her excuse for her own failure. Now she's back at square one."

That was true. What she hoped she would get from Ethiopia and Kassahun must have been no better than what she had before, and the heart of her agony, her desire to water the talent she felt was dessicating, must not have lessened.

We left the story for awhile. It could have ended then. But we heard later that Kassahun had gone to the States.

"Tekle Ibrahim says Kassahun left a week ago," Roger announced. "The ticket arrived from Corinne herself. Tekle says Kassahun had been waiting for it all along!"

"But how? What happened—I mean her breakdown? You don't suppose in your wildest imagining that the breakdown was an act? To get Peace Corps to pay the way?

"But of course you see, don't you?" I said, "It's *she* who's won."

"You sure?"

This final act offered me that possibility. She had held. And, more to the point, was rising, if Kassahun meant anything at all.

A pledge had been honored. The drama had proportion now. She, like Malfi, like the Duchess herself, would *be*.

Alemé's story came later. She claimed that Corinne and Sid had invited her to live with them. Corinne wanted her for Sid. Alemé had pulled away and in the dark hallway of the villa had whispered to Kassahun, staring into his black eyes "*Min aynet!* Just what is this?" But he hadn't said a word. The story, because of Alemé's refusal, made poor Sid a cuckold and little more, and Corinne, well, a sort of madame. Did this mean we had to rewrite the whole thing? They had been gone so long, we barely could recall what we had constructed around them so far, what themes had survived our revisions.

"She wasn't sure," Roger suggested, "how far he'd let her go, so she tempted him with Alemé. Kassahun and she weren't enough. It proved nothing. Once he went with Alemé, then she had him."

"Yes, I see," I whispered, "she saw he didn't care about *her* infidelity. She was daring him with something else—a betrayal."

"You mean him, betraying her?"

"His vision of her. The person he wanted her to be. His view of her was a thousand miles off. It was killing her. She couldn't compete with the image."

"You think she wanted him to take her the way she was or not at all?"

"No, she was done with him. But she wanted him to betray his illusion, spit on his own dream. Shitcan it. She needed to ruin him."

"The question still is," Roger asked, "what was she after? Freedom? I don't think she ever wanted that. She'd have dared nothing without Kassahun."

"Actually, she probably didn't have an end in mind. I mean, it was endings she was fighting. The one she saw looming in Colorado was enough."

That is how we left it for the time. They have been gone at least six months now. But I keep expecting to see Kassahun return. Or perhaps I might even spot her coming toward me through the cold air of morning again. She said she wanted to emigrate.

And we will probably go on some more with our tellings. There's still so much to figure out. We need to uncover some secret that will make the story solid. What surprises me still is how this mystery lingers in the traces they left behind. Why, only this morning I saw a white woman wearing Ethiopian dress, her head covered. She passed close to me and I could smell her perfume. I must have stared, for at the corner she turned to look at me, the angle of her head an invitation. From the distance the pale soft shawl looked like long hair let fall, thick and clean, to her waist, her eyes large and dark, staring.

Transformed, she sat on a rock somewhere singing softly, her hands and tail marking circles in the water while her lover watched from some fantastic shore in disbelief.

ETHIOPIA

Parking in Washington sometimes feels like destiny. In our family we shop where we park and choose our restaurants that way. One day, about a year ago, my son and I got a spot in Georgetown near a Middle Eastern take-out called the Fast Fetoosh which had gyros and pads of thick pita breads in the window, bowls of shredded lettuce and chopped tomatoes, yogurt laced with cucumber and garlic the way we like it. Inside, there was a stand-up bar with a few stools pressed along the back wall and against a large mirror. We saw shakers of oregano and parmesan, red crushed pepper, images in duplicate, their reflections in a line. And the shadow, doubled, of a black woman, leaning, lighting a cigarette. I told the cook we'd eat our gyros there and when I turned, I saw the black woman had an Ethiopian face and it was someone I had known twelve years before in Addis Abeba.

If you ask people who have ever lived in Ethiopia, they tell you that you never put it behind you. During Peace Corps training there in 1971, the word was that Ethiopia had the highest dropout rate among trainees, but it also had the highest extension rate of any country in the world. Which meant that if you stayed, you never wanted to leave. And after you left, all you wanted to do was go back, and when you couldn't get there, you found Ethiopians on the outside, or they found you, or you found each other across the world like this, as if by magic.

"My God! I know you!" I said. Her name was coming to me slowly, not as fast as the other impressions because she had been a story and more than that, part of the imaginary life I had there in which I made her up, a fiction, trying to piece together who she was with who I was, as if our lives had joined in some continuum outside of time and space. I had fixed on her because she had this scar that ran from the end of her eyebrow down the left side of her face as though she had been cut in a violent episode. It must have been a deep slash, now a faint path a half inch wide but clean: there were no other marks at all on her face. It gave a depth to her beauty and to me, a million stories.

"Your name is Tsegaynesh, isn't it?" I said. In Amharic it means "you are my grace." She was looking at me, trying to remember and I was talking fast, stumbling over the connection.

"Yes, I lived in Addis. In the Peace Corps. You remember that guy, that Swedish guy, Tony? Tony, the Swede?"

It was impossible, really, that we could have met like this on the basis of that parking space: there was a cosmic feel to it, if you weren't giddy and laughing, holding that oily, overflowing sandwich. "I just *do not* believe this." Which was true.

She was laughing, too. She had such luck, and in a country as big as America, in a city like Washington, to find someone, anyone, even if she didn't actually remember them. "Only my name is *Tse-hai-nesh.*"

"Tse-hai-nesh," I repeated carefully. "You. Are. A. Sun?" But she was spelling it for me on my napkin with a pen.

"You know Amharic?"

"Well, I did once." I wished I could have unlocked that compartment in my brain and talked and talked from that other soul.

"Tony, that Swedish guy, his dog bit my kid Rafe." Who was now six feet tall and standing there eating as if such things happened every day.

"So he wanted to make up for it by taking us out to dinner. You were there. I don't remember where we went."

"Oh yes," she was faltering, but she did know who Tony was. "Tony. He made films."

"That's the one."

I had seen her from time to time after that dinner with Tony. Addis Abeba was a city of outdoor cafés where people met by chance, and sometimes I met Tsehainesh and we would drink coffee. Once, I don't remember why, she took me to her house. We walked.

Clusters of compounds, houses behind gates, were scattered at random throughout the city. Everyone lived in compounds except the desperately poor who squatted between them in shanties, or settled down into the ridges that drained the many streams that ran through Addis Abeba. Sometimes you went over dirt tracks through brush and trees, almost like forest, hardly aware of the walls surrounding the compounds until you saw the gates, the guards hunched near them in gray blankets or overcoats. Sometimes you went through streets and alleys dense with people and animals, flanked by butcher shops and kiosks and green grocers. Sometimes you had to go across the filthy ravines, the hillsides of falling shacks, through the stink of urine and burning dung, and the humiliated dogs.

Her house was in a compound high on a hill behind the English church. Not just the trees but the ground, bare of grass; the light, broken into fragments; the air, moist with rain, redolent of eucalyptus, made it seem that we were in a forest. It was an old house, painted so many times it had forgotten itself.

White now, it was lovely, with an Asian filigree of wooden porches and dark shutters, a crumbling staircase to a high front door. Inside it was cool and painted in dark colors. It was polished clean and smelled of roasted coffee and fresh Ethiopian spice, of old cement and wax. The furniture was simple, market pieces, cushions that had been covered and recovered and rugs that were worn. One chair sat perched on its broken legs. There was no junk around and the quiet seemed to echo down the long waxy halls. Windows opened as we entered and a voice called, *"Emete?";* someone had come in from a room out back.

We drank tea served by her maid, a girl no more than thirteen or fourteen. I wanted to wander through the house, to see all the rooms, their beds, their closets. I stood in the bathroom and looked in the mirror and thought for a moment I could see her face, and her mark—a child had fallen in a dark round house filled with smoke, against a machete left in the way. The glass was chipped and its mercury stained, the water cold on my hands and the soap. The towel was stiff, a remnant, washed and dried many times.

She had come from a village in the mountains to the west, out there where Ethiopia never ended, just rose and rose. Her mother, she told me, had never seen an airplane or a car. It amazed her: her own transformation. From the start hers was a kind of odyssey. Her father's favorite: he agreed to give her the chance and sent her off to high school. In town she was to live with an older man, one of her father's friends. Eventually, the man got the girl to sleep with him and she got pregnant. Her father came to kill them both. Instead, she had the baby, a boy, and the man took him and raised him. Tsehainesh left them and came down to Addis where she studied to be a nurse. She was no good at it, terrified of death, that someone would die while she had her hands on them. She met someone else, had two children. She wore slacks, drove a car and smoked. It was hard to be an Ethiopian woman, free like that, because everyone thought she was a whore, or worse. By the time I left Addis, she had opened a shop and was selling jewelry, a plan she had often talked about over the years.

"Are you here in America to stay now?"

"My daughters are here," she told me. "In California."

"And they let you out? And the Americans gave you a visa? I thought it was impossible for Ethiopians to get visas."

"It was easy. I only had to promise to go back."

"Will you?"

"No. No, I can't go back there. It's impossible."

"So you'll be a refugee then." I felt foolish, clutching this garlicky food that was too much with the tomatoes falling out of the pita.

"If I can get a green card," she said dreamily. "I only need to find a husband. Please, can you find one for me?" Which was almost, but not quite, a joke. I'd heard this business about husbands and wives and green cards before, these ruthless arrangements.

"A husband, eh?" Tastes mingled in my mouth to remind me of where I was.

"Yes. If you know someone. I can pay."

"I *still* can't believe this," I said because I couldn't. I was looking at my son who had finished eating.

"Yeah, it is insane really," he offered.

"So what are you doing now, here in Washington?"

She said, "I have some paintings. I want to sell them. Then I will start a shop. To bring Ethiopian art to this country. That's my idea."

"Paintings?"

"From my gallery. I had a gallery."

"And the jewelry business?"

"My God!" as though that was forgotten, an old dream. "Finished."

"So—paintings. Those paintings on goat skin?"

"Traditional paintings," she said. She used a somber, apologetic tone that Africans sometimes get when they talk about such things. "Why don't you come see them? I live just here."

There was no time. I took her address and her phone number and said I would come in a few days. We went out of the Fast Fetoosh together, arm in arm according to the form. There was a kind of joy in it, a sense made. It had to do with ideas I like to play with about such bizarre intersections, about the ways we know each other.

Ethiopia was more than memories for me, more than a distant place I'd lived in once. It was host to my first wild imaginings and to my first real disgust because to go there was to drop suddenly, not back in time to when men lived as primitives, romantic, close to Eden, but to an area that reflected, like a mirror, the real condition of our species. This was what was frightening: to see how fast you learned to live in the middle of misery as if it were inevitable, even necessary, a part of the natural order. It was like one of those old swarming tapestries or a Byzantine mosaic, a million pieces, fitted in the dome of a cathedral, a world neatly divided into levels, rising to heaven or sinking to hell. Angels: women in white veils, drifting, bowing, almost afloat, their voices high and sweet, smelling of perfumed smoke. One face more beautiful than the next. And fiends:

lepers strewn along a sweep of avenue, their limbs exposed, a child rushing toward you who has nothing left of his face. And dogs, whelped in ditches, thousands of dogs. You came across the clumps of puppies, squirming and mangy, a mother slung almost dead among them. A natural order that contained this beauty and horror as well as what has always been described as their fierce pride, the reflex of their isolation and blindness.

Ethiopia kept the sacred image of itself, its own icon. It was governed by some holy mathematic that I never figured out: the formulas for what you saw and what you looked away from. Rituals and secrets. After a while nothing was merely itself but grew to a symbol, took on more and more meanings as you held it and turned it in your mind, a language that thrived on ambiguity, words that revealed themselves as wax or gold, the profane and the sacred. It was amazing to me that in this strange setting we could keep the surface of our lives the way we did, days that went on as days do anywhere, in what now, as memory, seems to me like awe.

She was staying with a friend of a couple she had known in Addis. She knew so many people. She was someone who had learned to make her life from the people she collected, allowing them to be responsible. It was early in the afternoon and she was waiting for me, watching TV in a dark back room, wrapped in a heavy shawl. The house was cold and felt abandoned. She rubbed her hands as she answered the door.

"I hate to put on this heating," were her first words. "I need the fresh air."

All around the windows were open as if we were still on the equator.

First our hands extended, clasped, then came the embrace, then the kiss on each cheek, right-left-right, and the greetings exchanged in rhythm. *Tena-ystilin. Endemin nesh? Dehana neñ. Dehanan nesh? Dehanan ymesgin. Anchis? Dehana?* Getting past it, into it, like an old song. Making me sing, making me happy with it.

Right away she was asking, "Did you see it? Did you see last night on your television these pictures they are showing us now?"

She was talking about Mohammed Amin's film of the famine.

"We don't have a TV," I answered. "But I saw it in the paper this morning."

I wanted to say I was sorry. Her hair had been combed out and was wild and there was gray in it.

"I could take those pictures," she said. She was stepping back, drawing in the shawl. "Anywhere, anytime in Ethiopia. What are these pictures all of a sudden?" She sounded annoyed, a little weary as well. "It is our shame," making it seem a private, secret thing after all, a violation.

And I was a witness that she was running away from it. She was uncomfortable. Or frightened, or helpless. Just trying to survive her own life.

"What did anyone think was going on all these years? Are they so stupid?"

These were rhetorical questions: I knew the answers.

"They have taken our pride and given our country away—simply. These armies. To the Russians. To the Cubans. Who cares?"

I knew this was the worst of it: the famine had always been there.

"It's the same thing. Exactly like when we were there," I said. "The way they tried to hide the thing."

"Worse. A thousand times worse." She laughed. "You cannot believe it. Everyone is watching you. No . . . no, I can't, I can't . . ."

She wasn't talking about the famine now but about her own condition. And there was the bitter irony because we had wanted the emperor gone: nothing, we all said, nothing could be worse. Nothing. And now, we said, nothing but this.

She said, "Who was pointing fingers at Haile Selassie? Who? When *they* are worse?" She had a way of moving through a room as if there were an important destination on the other side. "Anyway, I'm fed up with politics," she called over her shoulder.

And there were the paintings which I had come to see. She brought them out, rolled and packed in long tubes, from the room where a game show droned.

"Ho! They're big enough."

We struggled with the tubes. I pulled, felt the cloth, the plastic texture of painted surface underneath, canvases rolled against themselves, like wishes.

"They are *beautiful!*" she sang, selling them to me if only she could. It made her breathless.

She believes in the fate that has stepped in and shaped her life, usually in the form of white foreigners. She believes in that parking space, and that we have met so I will be able to help her here. I saw all this in the way she unfurled those pictures.

"Queen of Sheba . . . Battle of Adwa . . . Saint George and the Dragon . . . ." Large canvases that thwacked against the floor. Mostly narratives, in the manner of old illuminated manuscripts, told like cartoon strips in framed scenes. They're paintings that are sold mostly to tourists.

I knew right away that she would have a hard time selling them in America: armchair travelers don't have the same pocketbooks as real ones who are dazzled by their journeys into buying anything. But I wasn't the person who was willing to tell her this. And it was clear she wouldn't listen either, not in the matter of her plans.

There were paintings that showed scenes from daily life. Traditional things, she might have said. Priests out with their elaborate umbrellas and filigree crosses. Weavers. Musicians. A woman hunkers by a fire brewing coffee. Raw meat is served to guests on platters. Like a school girl, I recited titles. We both felt like reminiscing and it almost worked the kind of magic you felt there, when you held small icons or old silver crosses in your hand; or saw people wrapped in white against the wind; boys with sheep braced on their shoulders, like Jesus, coming across dry plains or down yellow hillsides; and, amid the donkeys, low round houses, like dark cones, behind them in the distance. It almost worked: nostalgia's the veneer travelers fix over uncomfortable things.

"What do you think?" she asked me. "I must get a show."

"Where have you been with them?"

"Everywhere," she sighed. "It's impossible. No one will see me. They won't even look."

"You mean you've been going around, knocking on doors, saying I've got these pictures?" I was laughing. "Nah—they won't look at them. For one thing, they're not signed. And they're not old, so they should be signed."

She didn't quite believe me. "*I'll* sign them," she said, but realized that wouldn't work.

"Perhaps at craft shows or fairs," I said. "But galleries? I don't think . . ."

"Well then, I'll have to sell them privately."

She decided as though it were done. We both seemed lost in that room, among the pictures and the wind that came from the open windows.

That was the day I took her to a Goodwill Shop to find her a winter coat. She ran around through the racks and racks of clothes. Clothes heaped in bins and marked 50¢. Sweaters of all kinds, $1.00. Blue jeans. It seemed too good to be true: there were endless possibilities, and in our excitement, nothing looked too shabby or out of date. We tried things on. She ran to: blouses, skirts, jackets, shoes. Even torn things had the hope of repair. We must have stayed two hours, looking, trying. But in the end, she couldn't find anything she wanted.

Echoes: the touch of my friend's cheek against mine, the sound of Amharic, the images called back in the crude brush strokes of her canvases. There are so many Ethiopian restaurants on 18th street that walking there smells like Addis Abeba, of spices and fiery stews.

Akalewerk has called. We meet him anywhere at anytime in the patchwork way our lives are run. London once, at a party. Nairobi. Even in Lagos, Nigeria. Now he's in Washington doing whatever he does and has found our phone number in the book. He's on his way from Wisconsin to Zimbabwe where he'll work on a contract for FAO. He looks tired, a small man whose face could have come from a fresco high on the walls of a rock-carved church in Tigre. He was one who stayed in Ethiopia for as long as he could after the coup because he had wanted the revolution, like everyone else. He had believed in it, and in some ways, he'll say, he still does, despite everything, only it got too dangerous for him. No details: just too dangerous. He's more upset by what came over CBS the other night than Tsehainesh, perhaps because he'd been away for five years and in a state of denial, although he says, "Of course, everyone has known about this situation all along."

At which my husband nods. Of course. Was it fatalism or frustration these men shared, who are implicated by their knowledge, but innocent in every other way? J is obsessed by Ethiopia these days. For months he's been reading everything he can, in his office at USAID, every paper, national and international. Every cable. Every memo. So he, too, had known. Just as he had known in 1972. All along.

"Of course, they should be let to die." Akalewerk says this with conviction, though softly, whispering it. He's sitting on the edge of the couch and could have been a witness under oath.

"What is the point of having them continue in this endless misery?" he goes on. "Ruining the land? What is the meaning of such lives?"

To him right now that question doesn't seem as enormous as it is. To him right now the answer is clear. And who among us has any other answer that isn't too fragile to be exposed? He means what he's saying, I have no doubt, but I wonder whether it's because he values human life or doesn't. I'd be willing to swear that we were neurologically different at this point, if I didn't recognize the part of me that hears and understands what he's saying.

He wants to talk. There is a context after all and he's not a cruel or immoral man. On the contrary.

"When I was a boy," he says, "my father worked at the palace in the bodyguards. Once he was to travel to Sidamo and so invited me, his oldest, though I was *very* small." He could have been talking about another incarnation. "We both sat on the top of the truck, and, of course, we were looking down on the world. That was the first time I rode, by the way, so I can't forget it."

He flies everywhere in planes now.

"In each town where we stopped, they made us a feast. Killed a goat. Made honey beer. Outside at night, you saw the sky coming close. The stars. I was watching everything. There were many things that had no names."

His story calls up those nights in Africa when the sky comes alive with shooting things, stars or sparks, as if there were a spiral wind taking the world, houses, men, animals, up into the pitch.

"But you see," he says, "when we looked down, we saw trees so thick you could not see the ground. This is my point. Now if such a child should make that journey, he would see no trees at all. And that is only how many years since I was a boy?"

You don't want to hear the next step in this logic of the damned, so you say, slowly, hoping for an idea that will diffuse, "Yes, I know, but . . ."

"But what?" He was holding a rubber band and pulling it and letting it collapse. Perhaps it took three thousand years of isolation in those mountains to make a face like his which is, after all, perfect.

"You know," he bends to pick up something from the clutter on the floor, a small brass incense bowl, "when I was teaching at the college in Alamayu and there came Kolubi—you know Kolubi?—when all the lepers gather for the feast, their alms. Thousand and thousands of them, you don't believe it. And they are feeding them, as you know, this raw meat, and tea in tin cans. How they pick the bones until there is nothing, just pure white bones everywhere. And I was thinking, why don't they simply put some poison in that meat?"

Perhaps he's too mild a man to express his rage in any other way: his hand is white around that tiny bowl.

"Yes. You can't believe me, can you?"

He strikes the brass with his fingernail but it's dense and won't ring.

"Truly, that was my thought. It still is. If you cannot do anything else for them, then they should die. Surely you don't believe in God, do you?"

I admit that at times it is hard to do.

"But politics. You must believe in politics, as Americans. And if you feed them, as you will do, then Mengistu is off the hook, isn't he? So you will save him, not them, in the end."

Listening to him it could have been twelve years ago in another living room where outside the window we could see red bougainvillea covering a wall. He was talking about getting everyone out of northern Ethiopia and sealing the area off for maybe forty years until everything grew back. He had calculated the time based on something he read about a volcano in Korea that ruined everything, or perhaps it was Nagasaki, I forget. After the forty years, you let them back in. To him it was like war. Less drastic than what he was suggesting now but spoken out of the same despair, only now he's in exile, and if they are still his people or not seems to haunt him—has he betrayed them by leaving (to his advantage and their misery) and by wishing them all dead, always telling himself and anyone else who cares to know, that as soon as possible, as soon as it's safe, he's going home.

"So now *you* will be able to go there," he tells J. Either a joke or a challenge. He says it like a clairvoyant with an eyebrow raised. We're probably all conjuring the same vision now of what the scene will be: the rush to get the food in there, the bureaucracies screwing up, the system breaking down, the rumors of corruption. The politics.

"Not me." J's looking for a cigarette. He knows the pitfalls of famine relief. "I've done my share," he says. "In the Sahel. In Tanzania. I've done enough of it. It isn't what I ever wanted to do either." He's got lots of libelous stories about graft and mismanagement on all fronts, with himself in the middle, suspended in disbelief, trying to move papers. "Not me."

Akalewerk's smiling. "But won't they force you?" Placid, in the dark, solid ring of his hair.

The truth is that we've both been privately longing to go back, even now, more so now—out of curiosity and the tricks we play with ourselves about destiny because we all want one.

We had never intended to go to Africa in the first place: now it's the only place we want to go. We went to graduate school in New Mexico, learned Spanish, all with the idea of somehow getting down to Latin America. When the Peace Corps called from Washington and started talking about Ethiopia, we had to get out an encyclopedia. All that carrying on: my mother, whose name, perhaps prophetically, is Aida, came out wrapped in a sheet, making jokes about the lengths a man will go to get away from his mother-in-law. Ethiopia: on the globe you looked and saw how far away it was.

We told them no. But they persisted. A man named Glen Nichols who was on the staff there, practically begged J, an agricultural economist, promising him a position in the Ministry of Planning, a position that a man of forty with ten years experience might get any other place, a chance to get incredible experience, he said. And for me, a position in the Ministry of Education, an advisor on the High School English Curriculum for the whole country, all of which sounded curious, if not suspect, but we knew absolutely nothing at all, and like most people had a *National Geographic* view of Africa; wild animals and wilder tribes beating on drums and mostly naked. Nichols conned us into coming to Washington for an interview, and at a Mexican restaurant, he showed us pictures of Addis Abeba. The next day, down in the endless offices of the State Department, we saw a film.

Background music whined in a minor key. A voice talked from an encyclopedia about altitudes and longitudes, population statistics, geography and history. Ethiopia, it said, had the last ruling emperor in the world, the King of Kings, the Conquering Lion of Judah, a throne descending from Menelik, the legendary son of Solomon and the Queen of Sheba, the first Ethiopians. An African nation that had never been colonized. Three thousand years of independence. It talked about a form of Christianity going back to the fourteenth century, hidden in mountains from Moslem invaders, in churches carved out of the earth. They had never been conquered, though the Italians tried, the voice announced. While the camera gave us images: biblical, wild priests in saffron robes, rich embroideries, gold-trimmed umbrellas. Shepherd boys tending cows and goats, a village of round thatched huts, in landscapes of rising hills and mesas. Dust and shadows and sun. *Thirteen Months of Sunshine* was the title of the film. They used a lunar calendar, another time frame, that worked out to be eight years behind ours, so we would be going back to 1963.

What was behind that decision to join the Peace Corps? A family with a five-year-old boy? I'll never be sure. For me, part of it was an instinct opposite from the one that was settling everyone else down. It may have been the remnants of the ancient will to migrate which showed up as curiosity, a dream of other places, the way you gave yourself a chance. At bottom there was rebellion. From the beginning, when I started to go away, first to Italy, I wanted to flaunt it, as though crossing borders was a way of meeting the world's dare. And not to be a tourist either: you had to go and live someplace for months or years to make it real. You had to learn the language which offered a kind of freedom, another way of saying things, another psyche. To know how an Ethiopian will express this or that, constructions that make you sound a stranger to yourself, let you be someone else.

And for J? I didn't know it then: he's a fundamentalist, but without religion or hysteria, save his own brand that has its source in common sense and independence. He's a man who'll never pay interest to borrow money, and he'd feel rage paying off a mortgage on a house that someone else had built. Even then it looked as though our country was headed in another direction. We may have flattered each other into poses of idealism—to help the poor as volunteers—but I think the truth was that we were both looking for a way to avoid what America wanted us to be. To look for other forms of responsibility. And then, of course, there was this promise of adventure: the experimental mode, tossing into uncertainty a bottle, with a message washing ashore.

It does an ego good, this process of self-election. We made it sound like a mission, somewhere down in D.C. in a steakhouse where they gave you all the salad you could eat, all the beer you could drink. A waitress, laughing, brought it to us in pitchers.

From the table next to ours, an eavesdropper, who was also meeting the challenge, said, "Go. Wherever the hell it is you're talking about. Just go. Excuse me for listening." He paused, grinning, leaning forward; his necktie strained. "Just pack 'er up and *go!*" as if he were setting a caged bird free, or he was Moses on the shore. We told Glen Nichols we would go.

Now, fourteen years later we were making the same decision again. This time it wasn't a film called *Thirteen Months of Sunshine* we were looking at but pictures of a famine. Akalewerk had seen, that night the first pictures were aired on CBS, what became inevitable, that Americans would be going back to Ethiopia, and that J would be asked to be one. It took a year to say yes. It should have been easier. There were a lot of memories at stake, and most of our friends are in exile. The regime appeared, from all reports, to be criminal, at times ridiculous. Still, there are people who have told us we'll find everything curiously, even ominously, the same. A little poorer, a little sadder, a little more alone. One tyranny, after all, has only replaced another. Others have different stories, because after three thousand years, Ethiopia finally has been conquered and beaten down by outsiders. "They have taken our pride and given our country away."

I would have gone right back, but I think J needed the year to sort out his terms. In the meantime there was too much hysteria. The congregation at my mother's church was asked to bring in canned goods to feed the starving. A company in Texas had called J's office offering to send gallons and gallons of liquid fertilizer to help, as though Ethiopia were a kind of house plant. Rock bands and movie stars. Airlifts of Falasha. J was waiting for the moment to fade: it made more sense to someone with his sensibilities to go when it was quieter and ripe for repair, when the mad rush was over and there were farmers again, trying to plant food.

I told Tsehainesh, "I'm going to hire you to teach me Amharic again."

"So! You will go then?"

She would be jealous. She was homesick. She still had no job and her papers, asking for asylum, were temporary. She had tried to be a waitress, one lunch hour in a huge restaurant, but the subway fares were more than she could earn. For two weeks she had been the companion of a very rich, old lady, but the idea of a refugee had scared the old woman—her jewels and her silver and her failing sight. She still had her paintings and she still was talking about selling them to get a stake. She still was asking me if I knew someone who would marry her. Her exile had become a huge, unwieldy thing.

I didn't have any Amharic books so we had to do our lessons from scratch. I had to teach her how to teach me so she won't be tempted to translate or try to explain. I told her to simulate, the way a child learns. It seemed impossible that there was a time I knew this language well. Now I can't make sentences or converse at all. Marvellously, the words are still there: they came suddenly without reason, even without their meanings. "*Yimesliñal?* What does that mean? *TebeKñ?*" What made us laugh is that the connections are missing, the tissue of context and grammar that will let me talk instead of just spout these random words.

We go around the room with nouns and the room changes,

stirring like memory. *Womber. Terrapeza.* I wonder what it will be like in a few weeks time, landing in Addis Abeba again, if the connections will all come back to make the picture clear. I remember vividly though, still, how the plane came in low over the land, we saw hills like waves on a choppy sea, the land cut up into plots, the conical rooftops. It was the rainy season and I had never seen such green.

ABOUT THE AUTHOR

Maria Thomas was the pen name of Roberta Worrick. She was born July 6, 1941 to Robert R. and Aida Thomas in New Jersey, grew up in Ohio and Massachusetts and graduated from Mt. Holyoke College in 1963. She studied painting in Florence, then taught English at a boarding school in Vermont, and married Thomas Worrick. She taught at New Mexico State and earned an MA in English from Penn State. In 1971, she and her husband, an agricultural economist, joined the Peace Corps and went, together with their young son, to Ethiopia.

After Ethiopia, the Worricks moved on to Nigeria, Tanzania and Kenya. In each country, Maria became interested in local art, culture and languages. She began to write stories based on the expatriate experience. Her early work was published in periodicals such as *Redbook, North American Review* and *The Antioch Review.* She won the *StoryQuarterly* Fiction Prize, *Chicago Review* Annual Fiction Award and a National Magazine Award for several of the stories later collected in *Come to Africa and Save Your Marriage* (Soho Press 1987). She was awarded a Wallace E. Stegner Fellowship for the year 1987 by Stanford University.

In April 1987 her novel *Antonia Saw the Oryx First* was published to acclaim. In that year she also won the Overseas Press Club's Commendation for her reportage on the Ethiopian crisis which had appeared earlier that year in *Harper's.*

She returned to Africa in 1988, first to Liberia and then to Ethiopia where her husband was engaged in relief work on behalf of the United States.

The Worricks accompanied a congressional mission, headed by Congressman Mickey Leland, to inspect a refugee camp on the Ethiopia-Sudan border. On August 7, 1989 their airplane crashed. There were no survivors.